It was tiresome to know so little about the doctor.

"I really must find out," said Louisa, talking to herself since there was no one else to talk to.

"What must you find out, Miss Howarth?" The doctor's voice, so quiet behind her, took her by surprise so that she choked on her scone, coughing and spluttering while he thumped her back.

When she at last caught her breath, she said indignantly, "What a beastly thing to do, creeping up on me like that...."

He said gravely, "I do apologize. I had no idea you were of a nervous disposition."

Not an answer to soothe her already ruffled feelings!

Betty Neels spent her childhood and youth in Devonshire, England, before training as a nurse and midwife. She was an army nursing sister during the war, married a Dutchman and subsequently lived in Holland for fourteen years. She lives with her husband in Dorset, England, and has a daughter and grandson. Her hobbies are reading, animals, old buildings and writing. Betty started to write on retirement from nursing, incited by a lady in a library bemoaning the lack of romantic novels.

Books by Betty Neels

HARLEQUIN ROMANCE®

Don't miss any of our special offers. Write to us at the following address for information on our newest releases.

Harlequin Reader Service
U.S.: 3010 Walden Ave., P.O. Box 1325, Buffalo, NY 14269
Canadian: P.O. Box 609, Fort Erie, Ont. L2A 5X3

BETTY NEELS
An Ideal Wife

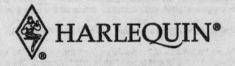

TORONTO • NEW YORK • LONDON
AMSTERDAM • PARIS • SYDNEY • HAMBURG
STOCKHOLM • ATHENS • TOKYO • MILAN • MADRID
PRAGUE • WARSAW • BUDAPEST • AUCKLAND

ISBN 0-373-03647-7

AN IDEAL WIFE

First North American Publication 2001.

Copyright © 1998 by Betty Neels.

CHAPTER ONE

IT WAS six o'clock on a glorious June morning and the sun was already shining from a blue sky. But it wasn't sunshine which woke Louisa, it was a persistent thumping on the door knocker and presently the doorbell.

She sat up and peered at the clock by the bed. Far too early for the postman, and the milkman had no reason to make such a racket. She turned over and closed her eyes, still not quite awake, and then shot up in bed as the knocker was thumped again. She got out of bed then, flung on a dressing gown and went quickly downstairs. Whoever it was must be stopped before her stepmother was awakened, besides, neighbours living decorously in the quiet little street would complain.

She unbolted the door and was confronted by a man tall and broad enough to blot out the street beyond him. She had the impression of good looks and angry blue eyes as he spoke.

'And about time, too. Must I stand here for ever, banging on your door?'

'Not unless you want to. Are you drunk or something? It's barely six o'clock in the morning.'

He didn't look drunk, she reflected. His clothes were casual—trousers and a thin pullover—and he needed a shave. Louisa, who had a vivid imagination, wondered if he was an escaped prisoner on the run.

'What do you want?' she added stupidly. 'And go away, do.'

'I do not want anything and I am only too anxious to go away, but if you will look behind that bay tree beside the door you will see someone whom I presume belongs to you. She was half in and half out of your gate.'

Louisa nipped down the steps and peered round the tub. 'Oh, Lord, it's Biddy.'

She glanced at the man. 'Our housekeeper.' She bent to touch Biddy's cheek. 'She's all right?'

'She appears to be suffering a severe migraine. Be good enough to open the door wide and I will carry her in.'

Louisa pattered ahead on her bare feet, down the elegant little hall, into the kitchen and through the door at the end into the spare room. She flung back the counterpane and covered Biddy after he laid her on the bed.

'I'd better get our doctor...'

'No need. Let her sleep it off.'

He was already walking away, and she hurried to keep up with him.

'Well, thank you very much. It was kind of you to stop. I hope it hasn't made you late for work.'

He didn't answer, only walked through the hall and out of the door without looking round.

'You have no need to be so ill-tempered,' said Louisa, and closed the door smartly on his broad back. If she had stayed for a moment she would have seen him cross the street and get into the Bentley standing there, but she went back to see Biddy, putting the kettle on as she went.

An hour later Louisa went upstairs to dress. Biddy

would be fit for nothing for quite a few hours; Louisa would have to wake her stepmother before she left for work and break the news to her that she would have to get her own breakfast.

Downstairs once more, Louisa crammed down cornflakes and tea while she got early morning tea for her stepmother and then nipped upstairs once again.

Her stepmother's bedroom was shrouded in semi-darkness, cluttered with discarded clothes and redolent of an overpowering scent. Louisa pulled back the curtains and put her tray down beside the bed.

She said, 'Good morning, Felicity,' in a voice nicely calculated to rouse the supine figure on the bed. 'Biddy isn't well. She's in bed, and I don't think she'll feel well enough to get up for the rest of the day. I've brought you your tea and laid breakfast for you in the kitchen.'

Mrs Howarth moaned softly and dragged herself up against her pillows.

'Louisa, must you come bouncing in like this? You know how delicate my nerves are. And what's all this about Biddy? Of course she's not ill. How am I supposed to manage without her? You'll have to stay home...'

Louisa looked at her stepmother who was still an attractive woman, even with her hair in rollers and no make-up. 'Sorry. Sir James is booked solid all day and his nurses won't have a moment to answer phone calls and check in the patients. You can go out to lunch. I'll be home around six o'clock, and we can have a meal then. I dare say Biddy will be all right again by tomorrow. A migraine,' said Louisa.

'You could have brought me my breakfast,' complained Mrs Howarth.

'I'm just off,' Louisa told her. 'I'll take a quick look at Biddy before I go.'

Biddy was awake, feeling sorry for herself. 'Miss Louisa, I dunno how I got here…'

'Well, you got as far as the gate,' said Louisa. 'Someone passing saw you and thumped the knocker.'

'The missus didn't hear?'

'No, no. I told her that you were very poorly. Once your head's better, you'll be quite yourself again.'

'Bless you, Miss Louisa. I got an awful 'eadache.'

'Yes, but it will get better, Biddy. Try and go to sleep again. I've put some milk here by your bed and some dry biscuits.' She stooped and kissed the elderly cheek. 'Poor old Biddy. I must fly or I'll get the sack.'

'You ought not to be working,' said Biddy. 'There's money enough; spends it all on herself, she does. It ain't fair.'

'Don't worry about it, Biddy. I like my job, and I meet lots of interesting people.'

'You ought ter 'ave a young man…'

'No time,' said Louisa cheerfully. 'Now, have another nap, Biddy, and don't try and get up—whatever Mrs Howarth says.'

Louisa caught her usual bus by the skin of her teeth, raced up Castle Street as fast as she dared without actually running, and hurried through the dignified portals of Sir James Wilberforce's consulting rooms. She heaved a sigh of relief as she opened the waiting room door; it was empty save for a pretty girl in nurse's uniform who was putting down the phone as Louisa crossed the room.

'You're late,' Jilly said unnecessarily. 'He wants you in there as soon as you arrive.' She added at Louisa's questioning look, 'He's in a good mood.'

Louisa tapped at the door of the consulting room and was bidden in Sir James's fruity voice to enter. He was standing looking out of his window, but turned to look at her as she went in. He was a short, stout man with a wealth of silver hair and a round face with small, bright eyes. His patients loved him despite his forthright manner.

He wasn't alone. The man standing beside Sir James turned when he did and gave Louisa a cool stare. Immaculate in his sober grey suit and silk tie, he looked very different from the man who had thumped the door knocker so fiercely that morning. Well, not different, thought Louisa, only the clothes. He was just as tall, his person was just as vast, and his eyes just as cold.

Sir James peered at her over his glasses. 'Good morning, Miss Howarth. I mustn't keep you from your work, but I must make you known to Dr Gifford. He is to become my part-time partner, taking over when I am on holiday or called away for any length of time. We shall see him once or twice a week, and you will work for him as you do for me.'

He beamed at her, and she realised that she was expected to show some sort of pleased acquiescence.

'I'll do my best,' said Louisa inadequately, and stared at Dr Gifford's waistcoat. 'How do you do?'

He said smoothly, 'I'm sure that Miss Howarth and I will work well together.'

Sir James said cheerfully, 'Oh, I'm sure you will. She is most reliable—a splendid worker. Not easily put out either.' He chuckled. 'Copes with emergencies...'

Louisa shot a look at Dr Gifford. He was smiling.

She didn't much care for the smile. She said rather
tartly, 'Fortunately, these occur very rarely.'

'Ah, well,' said Sir James cheerfully. 'One never
knows what lies round the corner. Thank you, Miss
Howarth; I expect you will wish to get on with your
work.'

Louisa murmured and slid away. For a big girl she
was very light and quick on her feet. Dr Gifford, listening gravely to his colleague's observations, considered her at his leisure. Big, but beautiful with it. All
that tawny hair piled up in a rather haphazard arrangement, that lovely face with its wide grey eyes, haughty
little nose and too large mouth which lifted at its cor-
ners, and a nasty temper when roused, he reflected.

Louisa went back to her desk and began the day's
work: answering the phone, booking patients, greeting
them with just the right amount of friendly sympathy
they hoped for, offering them cups of coffee, cheering
the faint-hearted, providing the social side of the practice while Mrs Grant, Sir James's head practice nurse,
dealt with the more tiresome aspects of it. They got
on well together, she and Louisa. Mrs Grant was a
motherly woman, and she was comfortably plump
with a bright rosy-cheeked face and iron-grey hair.

Louisa sat down at her desk, and since there were
no patients for the moment Mrs Grant popped out of
her little treatment room.

'Jilly's gone for coffee,' she said. 'She may be
pretty but, my goodness, she's slow. What was all that
about? Sir James introduced me to Dr Gifford; he
looks nice enough.'

'I'm sure he's a very pleasant kind of man,' said

Louisa, not meaning a word of it. 'Jilly must be delighted…'

Mrs Grant cast her a shrewd look. 'Jilly is delighted with anyone wearing trousers. I suppose a pretty face is good for the practice.' She smiled suddenly. 'You're pretty enough for several Jillys…'

Louisa said without conceit, 'But I'm big, aren't I? Men like wispy girls.'

Mrs Grant laughed. 'Not all of them, love. My Ronny settled on me, didn't he? And I'm not exactly sylph-like, am I?'

Jilly came back then, and Louisa, sitting watching her as she came into the room, had to admit that she was extremely pretty. Probably some of the younger patients, especially the men, found her very attractive.

'Well, what did you think of him?' she asked Louisa.

'Dr Gifford? Well, he must be a good man if Sir James wants him for a partner. We didn't speak, only to say how do you do.'

'Oh, I know he must be a good doctor,' said Jilly impatiently. 'But didn't you think he was frightfully good looking? And he smiled…'

'Why shouldn't he smile?' asked Louisa matter-of-factly, and then added, 'I must get on; Mrs Wyatt's due in five minutes.'

Jilly wasn't to be put off. 'Don't you like men? Haven't you got a boyfriend?'

'Well, of course I like men. And I do have a boyfriend. Now, do let me get on…'

She began sorting the morning's work—patients' notes, phone calls to make, accounts to deal with. She turned to the computer and stared into its blank face. She wasn't sure that Percy would like to be described as a boyfriend. It would be beneath his dignity, and smacked of a relationship which he would never tolerate. Nor would she, for that matter—not that he had ever asked her opinion.

Percy, an inch shorter than she was, would have liked to call her his 'little woman', only great strapping girls such as she could never be that. It was a pity that he had taken it into his head that her continued refusal to marry him was merely what he called 'womanly wiles'. Once or twice she had longed to give him a good thump and tell him to find some meek girl who wouldn't answer him back, but she had been well brought up—there were some things one just didn't do.

She sighed, and then smiled nicely as the next patient came in.

The last one went two hours later and Sir James went away to do his hospital rounds, taking Dr Gifford with him and leaving a pile of letters on Louisa's desk.

'See to that lot, Miss Howarth. Leave them on my desk and make out the cheques. Oh, and bank the cheques that have been paid, will you? I shall be back some time this afternoon.'

She watched Dr Gifford's broad shoulders disappear through the door; he had given her a thoughtful look and said nothing, but she hadn't expected him to. Before starting on the letters, she allowed herself to wonder if he disliked her. Hopefully she wouldn't see much of him. She wondered where he had a practice, and later, over their lunch sandwiches, she asked Mrs Grant if she knew.

'Didn't Sir James tell you? A country practice not too far from here. Blandford way. Took it over when his father retired. Very rural, apparently, but lovely country.'

She bit into a cheese sandwich. 'He's well thought of, so I'm told.'

'Married?' asked Jilly, pausing on her way home. She only worked in the mornings, and did that half-heartedly. Louisa thought that Sir James employed her because she was young and pretty and that was what the patients liked. That she was pretty herself, even if she was twenty-seven, was something she didn't regard.

'No, I don't think so,' said Mrs Grant. 'But don't waste your time on him, Jilly, he's as good as—to the Thornfolds' youngest daughter. It'll be a grand wedding.'

'Will she like being a GP's wife?' asked Louisa.

'If she loves him then she will,' declared Mrs Grant.

Not an easy man to love, reflected Louisa, and began to tidy up before going back to her desk.

When she got home again that evening she found Biddy on her feet once more, looking very much the worse for wear but nonetheless preparing dinner.

'Your Mr Witherspoon's coming,' she told Louisa. 'So the missus told me to do something special.'

'He's not mine,' said Louisa crossly. 'And why must he have something special?'

'Dunno, Miss Louisa. The missus is 'aving a rest; tired out after the 'airdresser's.'

Biddy spoke without rancour. Mrs Howarth was no longer young, but she was still very attractive, even beautiful when she had her make-up on and her hair freshly dressed. Louisa agreed cheerfully; she got on well enough with her stepmother although there was no affection between them. Felicity was selfish and lazy and extravagant, but she was easygoing, too, and good company, and she could be very appealing, with her charming smile and her look of helplessness. And she was small and slender so that Louisa always felt at a disadvantage—overlarge and clumsy, conscious of her generously built person.

It was a nuisance that Percy would be coming to dinner. He had begun to take it for granted that he was welcome whenever he chose to invite himself.

She had known him for some years, and really, she had to admit, there was nothing wrong with him. A young lawyer with a secure future, he was a bit on the short side but not bad-looking and an agreeable companion. But not for life—in ten years he would be pompous and, she suspected, mean with money. But her stepmother approved of him, and Louisa, for the sake of peace, had never told her that Percy had proposed several times and she had refused him. Not that that stopped him...

As she changed into a dress and piled her hair she decided that if he proposed again she would make him understand once and for all that she wouldn't marry him. She had never encouraged him, indeed she had discouraged him as nicely as possible without actually being rude. And a lot of good that had done...

Her stepmother was in the drawing room, leafing through a magazine. As usual she was beautifully dressed, her blonde hair expertly tinted, her face exquisitely made up. She looked up as Louisa went in.

'Hello, darling. Had a busy day? Why are you wearing that dull dress? It makes you look positively elderly. Whatever will Percy think?'

Louisa went to the window and opened it. It overlooked a small garden at the back of the house, and beyond that there was a splendid view of the cathedral spire. She said flatly, 'I don't dress to please Percy.'

She turned to look at her stepmother. 'Felicity, I don't intend to marry him, you know. He takes it for granted and so do you, and I've tried to be polite about it...'

'But, darling, he's so safe, and you would never have to worry about anything.'

'I don't want to be safe. I don't love him.'

'There are many things more important than love,' said Mrs Howarth sharply. 'Security and a nice house, holidays and decent clothes.'

'Is that why you married Father?' asked Louisa.

'I was very fond of your father,' said Mrs Howarth a bit too quickly. 'And, of course, before he lost that money we had a very pleasant home and I lacked for nothing.' She added wistfully, 'It's hard to live as I do now. Genteel poverty, I believe it is called.'

Louisa didn't reply. Her stepmother lived in some comfort and grudged herself nothing. She made no bones about accepting a generous slice of Louisa's salary for, as she pointed out in a reasonable voice, Louisa enjoyed living in the same comfort in a pleasant house, having Biddy to see to the running of it and eating the good food provided. The fact that Louisa did quite a lot of the housework, helped with the cooking and quite often did the shopping as well were facts which escaped her attention.

Louisa had asked her once how she would manage if she were to marry, and Mrs Howarth had said airily, 'Oh, my dear, I shall be quite all right; Percy will make sure of that.'

Watching him now, coming into the room, Louisa

remembered that. He was still in his thirties, but already staid and with a well-nourished look which she reflected would turn into a portly middle age. He was quite good-looking and very correct in his dress, and she knew that she could never marry him. He wasn't her kind of man. Her kind of man was utterly different. A sudden memory of Dr Gifford took her by surprise and she blushed faintly, which was unfortunate as Percy took it as a compliment for his appearance.

He had brought flowers with him and a bottle of wine, which he offered with a smug smile, confident of his thoughtfulness and their gratitude.

He kissed the cheek Mrs Howarth offered and crossed the room to where Louisa was standing by the window. 'Hello, old lady—that's a charming dress, and you're as beautiful as ever.'

Old lady, indeed! She turned her cheek so that his kiss barely brushed it, and took the carnations he offered. She said, 'Thank you for the flowers, Percy,' and then added, 'I'll go and see if Biddy wants any help.'

When she had gone, Mrs Howarth said placatingly, 'She's shy, you know. I'll leave you together after dinner.' They smiled at each other, and as Louisa came back into the room they began to discuss the weather.

Biddy, still with something of a headache, had done her best, but the soup was too salty, the lamb chops slightly charred and the pudding bore a strong resemblance to a deep-frozen dessert. Percy, who prided himself on being a gourmet, ate with an air of martyred distaste while he enlarged at some length upon the political situation.

Louisa, brought up by an old-fashioned nanny, assumed her politely listening face and said, 'Really?' or 'Is that so?' at intervals, which was all that Percy required; the sound of his own voice was sufficient for him.

Louisa, munching petits pois which had been over-cooked, allowed her thoughts to wander. Where did Dr Gifford live? she wondered. She didn't like him, she reminded herself, but he looked interesting.

She caught Percy's eye and made the mistake of smiling at him, and her stepmother said at once, 'We'll have coffee in the drawing room. I'll go and tell Biddy.'

'I'll go,' said Louisa, hopeful of a few minutes' respite from Percy's ardent gaze.

'No, no, dear. Take Percy along to the drawing room and I'll join you in a moment.'

The drawing room was a pleasant place, and the very last of the sun cast mellow shadows over its furniture. Louisa went to open another window and said over her shoulder, 'Sit down, do, Percy.'

But he had come to stand behind her, much too close for her liking.

'My dear girl, you have no idea how I have been longing to get you on your own. I've given you plenty of time to make up your mind, although I'm sure that you have done so already—after all, I'm not such a bad catch!' He laughed at his little joke, and Louisa ground her splendid teeth. 'I can manage to be free in September; we could marry then.'

Louisa slid away from him and sat down in a little Victorian crinoline chair. 'Percy, before you say another word, I *don't* want to marry you. If that sounds rude and unkind, I'm sorry, but it makes it clear, doesn't it? Once and for all.'

'Why not?' He sounded huffy but not heartbroken.

'I don't love you.'

He laughed. 'You silly girl, of course you do. Only you won't admit it.'

She stared at him. How did one make anyone as conceited as Percy understand something they didn't want to know?

'No, I don't. If I did, I would have said so ages ago.' She added, 'I'm sorry to disappoint you, Percy. We've known each other for a long time, haven't we? And we can still be friends, if you wish. You'll meet a girl who'll fall for you, and you'll be happy ever after.'

Percy stood in the middle of the room, looking at her. 'I have no wish to be your friend,' he said ponderously. 'Indeed, from what I have seen of your present behaviour, I consider that you would be quite unworthy of my friendship.'

Louisa goggled at him. He sounded like someone out of a Victorian novel, only worse. She said briskly, 'Oh, well, that settles that, doesn't it? Will you stay for coffee?'

It was entirely in character that he should agree. Anyone else—any man—other than Percy would have made some excuse and cut short the evening. But not Percy. His coffee, apparently, was more important to him than any awkwardness she might be feeling.

'Well, if you are going to stay, sit down,' she begged. 'Isn't the weather glorious? I love June, don't you? Not too hot and the garden beginning to look lovely—if you have a garden.'

Percy sat, arranging his trousers just so, in order that the creases wouldn't be spoilt. 'You have no need to make conversation, Louisa. I am deeply hurt, and trivial talk is hardly going to assuage that.'

Only Percy could talk like that. Why hadn't she noticed that before? Perhaps because she had known him for so long.

She said flippantly, 'I thought it was the girl who felt hurt.'

He gave her a look. 'Only you, Louisa…'

He was interrupted by Mrs Howarth's entry, with Biddy behind her carrying the coffee tray.

'You've had your little talk?' she asked. 'Always so nice to clear the air.'

'Oh, we've done that,' said Louisa promptly. 'I've finally persuaded Percy that I won't do for his wife.'

Mrs Howarth gave a little trill of laughter. 'Oh, darling, isn't it time that you stopped being hard to get? Percy has had the patience of a saint…'

Louisa took the tray from Biddy and set it down on the small table beside her stepmother's chair. 'Felicity, you've been reading too many old-fashioned novels. I'm not a shrinking damsel of seventeen, you know.' She looked at Percy. 'I expect that's the reason that I don't want to marry you, Percy. I'm too old for you, and I don't know how to shrink!'

'I don't understand you, Louisa. Such flippancy about a solemn thing such as marriage.' He held out his cup for more coffee. 'I find the whole conversation distasteful.'

'You do? So do I, but I'm glad we've had it. I thought I knew you very well, but not well enough, it seems. Now I do.'

Mrs Howarth spoke sharply. 'Louisa, how can you be so unkind to Percy? Really, I'm quite shocked and upset.'

'Well, I can't think why,' said Louisa sensibly.
'I've told you that I have no wish to marry Percy.
And I've told him a dozen times.'

Percy got to his feet. 'It is better that I do go, I
think.' He managed to sound sad and yet at the same
time maintained what Louisa took to be a stiff upper
lip.

'Never mind, Percy. You're well rid of me, you
know.' She offered a hand and he took it reluctantly
and heaved a sigh.

'I shall always have happy memories of you,
Louisa—until today, of course.'

He took a sorrowful leave of Mrs Howarth then,
and Louisa went to the front door with him. She
should be feeling guilty, she supposed, but what she
felt was a sense of freedom.

When she went back to the drawing room her stepmother said angrily, 'You're a fool, Louisa. You're
not a young girl any more; you can't afford to be
choosy.'

'Yes, I can. I've a nice job, and on my next birth-
day I get grandmother's money that she left me. I can
be independent for as long as I wish.' She paused.
'Tell me, Felicity, did Percy know about that—my
legacy?'

Mrs Howarth looked uncomfortable. 'Well, you
know how things slip out...'

'It would have been useful to him, wouldn't it?
Happy young bride hands husband a nice lump sum
so that he can shoot ahead in his career. Or was he
going to persuade me to make some of it over to you?'

'I don't know what you're talking about, Louisa. I
have been left very comfortably off by your father.'

'You're overdrawn at the bank. You forget, you

told me to open the post for you the other morning.
There was a letter from the bank manager...'

'You had no right.'

'No, I know that. I didn't read it deliberately; the
letter was folded in such a way that I couldn't help
but read it as I took it out of the envelope.'

Mrs Howarth said in a wheedling voice, 'Louisa,
dear, it's only temporary. If you could let me have
some money? I'll pay you back.'

'Have you paid Biddy?'

'Oh, she doesn't mind waiting. She hasn't anything
to spend her money on, anyway.'

'How many weeks do you owe her?'

'A couple—well, three, I suppose.'

'I'll pay Biddy's wages for three weeks. I dare say
you can borrow whatever you want from one of your
friends.'

'Oh, I couldn't possibly—I play bridge with most
of them, and how could I ask them here for lunch?'

'Then don't ask them,' said Louisa. 'Try Percy. I'm
going to see Biddy, then I'm going to bed.'

Biddy was tidying the kitchen before going to bed.
Her eyes brightened at the sight of the notes Louisa
held out to her.

'Well, now, Miss Louisa, the money will be very
welcome—got ter think of me old age, 'aven't I?'

'Of course, Biddy. And if you don't get your wages
regularly, will you let me know and I'll remind Mrs
Howarth?'

Louisa went to bed then, but not to sleep at once.
She sat by the open window of the pretty room and
thought about her future. It seemed obvious to her that
Felicity would be better off without her—she might
marry again, for she was still pretty and amusing. It

would be best if she found a room, or a tiny flat somewhere in the city not too far from Sir James's rooms.

She would miss the comfortable life she led now,
but that didn't worry her particularly. Indeed, she had
always wished to live independently but her stepmother had begged her to stay. She could see that if
she stayed now she would be in a rut from which there
would be no escape. A place of my own, thought
Louisa with satisfaction, and when I get Granny's
money I'll find a flat, somewhere near the cathedral.

She settled down to sleep then, her mind made up.
Of course, there would be difficulties with Felicity,
although probably she would be relieved not to have
Louisa around the house. Louisa had a little money
saved, and the money she currently paid Felicity each
week would go towards the rent of rooms. A pity she
had no one to advise her. Dr Gifford, for instance.
She came wide awake at the thought. He was the very
last person she would wish to receive advice from!

Mrs Howarth sulked for several days and gave vent
to her annoyance by going shopping, buying expensive clothes on her credit cards, spending long hours
with friends, playing bridge and gossiping. She ignored Louisa when she was home; this had no effect,
though, for Louisa had her pretty head filled with
ideas and schemes.

She had gone to various estate agents and enquired
about flats, and had been appalled at the rents of even
the smallest ones. Of course Salisbury, being a cathedral city, had a certain prestige, and the area around
the close where she would have liked to live was very
expensive. She began to hunt around streets further

afield, where the rents were within her means, but she found nothing to suit her.

It was when she took Biddy into her confidence that her luck changed. 'A flat?' asked Biddy. 'Bless you, Miss Louisa, there's Mrs Watts—I see 'er down at the Bell regular. Told me she 'ad a nice little flat. One of those little turnings off St Anne's Street. Close by and very quiet, so she tells me.'

'Do you suppose she would consider me, Biddy? If I were to go with you on your evening off we could meet her at the Bell.'

Biddy considered. 'Well, now, it ain't the place for a pretty young lady ter be. But there's a snug at the back of the bar; I dare say we could arrange something. Leave it ter me; I owes yer, Miss Louisa. I'll miss yer, but it don't seem right that you should do more than your share. I know you go out a bit with the missus, but only to dull bridge parties and the like. You needs young people—a man. Like 'im 'oo carried me ter me room. Mind you, I didn't see 'im all that clearly but 'e was a big chap and 'e 'ad a nice voice.'

She peeped at Louisa. 'Seen 'im again, 'ave you, Miss Louisa?'

'Well, yes. He came to Sir James's rooms one morning. He's a doctor.'

'Ah.' Biddy was all at once brisk. 'Well, I'll 'ave a chat with Mrs Watts and let you know, Miss Louisa.'

As ill luck would have it, Biddy's next free evening was forfeited. Mrs Howarth had issued invitations for dinner and bridge afterwards to several of her friends, and Biddy had to be on hand to cook and serve the meal.

'I don't suppose it matters to you when you have your evenings,' she'd told Biddy. 'I shall be out to dinner on Saturday, so have it then.'

Despite this setback, Louisa decided that it was a good thing. If her stepmother was out to dinner, then they wouldn't need to worry about getting back before the Bell closed. Mrs Howarth had told Louisa sulkily that she could have the house to herself or go out with any of her friends.

'It's Biddy's night off so you'll have to get your own meal. I dare say you'll manage. It's as well you're not invited; Percy will be there.'

'Just as well,' agreed Louisa sweetly. 'And don't worry about me. I hope you have a pleasant evening.'

The Bell was old, dark-beamed and crowded. Biddy led Louisa through the groups of people clustered in the bar and into the snug behind it.

Mrs Watts was already there, sitting at a small table with a glass of stout before her. She was a small woman, very thin, and could have been any age between forty and fifty years old. But she had a friendly face and manner, and after the ladies had had their refreshment the three of them walked the short distance to her house. It was indeed small, the front door opening onto a tiny hall and the narrow staircase enclosed by another door.

'I live downstairs,' said Mrs Watts. 'Come up and see if it suits you.'

There were two very small rooms, a tiny kitchen and shower room and loo, all very clean, and the furniture, although basic, was well cared for. There was a view of the cathedral from the sitting room window, and the roof beneath the window sloped down to the small garden below.

'If you are agreeable I'd very much like to rent it,' said Louisa. 'It's just what I was looking for. If I pay you a month's rent in advance and move in gradually?'

'Suits me. Come and go when you like, though I don't want any of those rowdy parties. Not that that's likely; Biddy has vouched for you being a young lady who is quiet and tidy.' She smiled. 'Not that I've any objection to a young man paying a visit.'

'I haven't one,' said Louisa cheerfully. 'But there's always hope.'

She looked round the little place again. 'May I have a key?'

'Course you can. Two—one for the front door and one for this flat. One month's notice on either side?'

'Yes. Do we have to write that?'

'No need. I won't do the dirty on you.' Mrs Watts drew herself up to her full height. 'I'm an honest woman.'

'Me too, Mrs Watts. I'm so pleased to have found this flat; it's Biddy's doing, really. I'll start bringing a few things round next week; I'm not sure when I shall actually move in.'

CHAPTER TWO

LOUISA told her stepmother of her plans as they walked back from morning service at the cathedral. Mrs Howarth was in a good mood; she was wearing a new outfit which she knew suited her, and she had spent some time talking to friends after the service, arranging to meet at a coffee morning later in the week at which there would be a well-known TV personality.

'Someone I've always wanted to meet,' she told Louisa. 'Such a handsome man. If he's staying here in Salisbury I might invite him to dinner.'

She glanced up at Louisa, strolling along in her plain crêpe dress with its little jacket. The girl has an eye for decent clothes, reflected Mrs Howarth, and she is quite lovely. A pity she is so large. 'I dare say you might like to meet him, Louisa.' She added quickly, 'Of course, we would have to have a specially nice meal. Perhaps you'd help out? My monthly cheque hasn't come...'

It seemed the right moment. Louisa said in a matter-of-fact way, 'Well, I can't. I've found a dear little flat—it's about five minutes' walk from us. I've taken it and I'm moving in as soon as I've collected my bits and pieces.'

Mrs Howarth stopped short. 'You can't, Louisa. What am I to do? How shall I manage on my own?'

'You won't be on your own; there's Biddy. And I

have mentioned several times that if I found somewhere I liked I'd wish to have my own place.'

'I'm very upset. You're being most unkind.' Mrs
Howarth turned a carefully wistful face to the troublesome girl. 'How was I to know that you meant
what you said?'

'Well, I usually do, don't I?'

'Your father wouldn't have approved...'

Louisa stared down at the cross face. 'Oh, yes, he
would.' She spoke patiently. 'You know as well as I
do that he would have wanted you to marry again,
and you'll have a far better chance without me; you'll
have no one to consider but yourself.' That had always been the case, but she didn't say so.

Felicity said thoughtfully, 'Well, yes, you may be
right. I have often refused invitations since it would
have meant leaving you on your own.'

Louisa took this remark with a pinch of salt, but
she said nothing and they walked on. At the house
Mrs Howarth said at last, 'Well, I suppose it's quite
a good idea. Of course, you must come here whenever
you want to.'

The matter settled, Louisa went round the house,
collecting up the odds and ends which were hers. Her
mother's little writing desk, the Georgian work table
she had inherited from her grandmother, some small
water colours and some of her father's books. And
Felicity, feeling generous, told her to choose what table lamps she might like to have.

So during the week Louisa went to and fro, gradually turning the little flat into a home, stocking the
kitchen cupboard and arranging for the milkman to
call, arranging for her post to be redirected, buying

some pretty cushions and, just before she moved in,
flowers.

She put her key in the door for the last time on
Friday evening, and on the following morning wished
her stepmother a temporary goodbye, spent half an
hour with Biddy in the kitchen, assuring her that she
was a mere five minutes away and that Biddy was to
come and have tea with her on her next day off, and
then she walked briskly away.

It was a lovely morning and the flat looked bright
and comfortable, the sunshine streaming through its
small windows. Louisa spent a happy day unpacking
her clothes, doing more shopping for food, and cooking herself an evening meal. She had wondered if she
would feel lonely, but that wasn't so. Indeed, she felt
free to do exactly what she wanted. No more bridge
parties and no more Percy...

All the same she went back during the following
week to make sure that Felicity wasn't feeling lonely.
She went during the evening after she had had her
supper, feeling guilty that she had been selfish in
wanting to have her own home. She need not have
worried. As she went into the house she could hear
the laughter and voices in the drawing room. The people turned to look at her as she went in—a party, a
rather noisy one, with drinks and delicious titbits and
her stepmother the centre of a group of her friends.
The look on her face when she saw Louisa made it
only too clear that she wasn't welcome, although
Felicity covered the look at once with a smile.

'Louisa, darling—how nice to see you! I'm having
a little party, just to cheer me up, you know? You
know everyone, I think?'

Louisa went round greeting people, spent a few

minutes with Felicity, and declared that she couldn't
stay as she was on her way to friends. A remark she
couldn't fail to see was a relief to her stepmother.

She didn't leave the house immediately, but went
to the kitchen where she found Biddy.

'Now here's a treat, Miss Louisa, and me just made
a pot of tea, too. Sit down and tell me how you're
getting on. Not lonesome?' She chuckled. 'The missus
is 'aving a 'igh old time; you don't need to worry
about 'er being lonely. Parties and bridge and jaunting
out to the theatre.'

Louisa said slowly, 'I should have done this sooner,
Biddy, and left her free to enjoy herself.' She caught
Biddy's anxious look and added, 'I'm very happy too,
really I am. I don't think I'm a very sociable person.'

'Well, as to that, Miss Louisa, perhaps you've not
met the right people you want to be sociable with.
But don't worry, 'e'll turn up...'

'Who?'

'Why, yer 'usband, of course. Just round the corner,
I dare say, waiting for yer—this year, next year...
some time—'

'Never,' said Louisa, and laughed. 'Don't you
worry about me, Biddy. I shall settle down nicely in
my little flat and enjoy the summer. There's the tennis
club, and the Walshes have asked me over whenever
I'd like to go; there's a swimming pool there.'

'Yer father liked them; their eldest boy's a bit older
than you are.'

'But not waiting round the corner for me, Biddy.
His eyes are fixed on Cecily Coates. I met her yesterday; they're as good as engaged.'

'Plenty of fish in the sea,' said Biddy.

Louisa went back to her flat, relieved that Felicity

was so happy but feeling hurt. She knew, had always known since the first time they had met, that Felicity had only a superficial liking for her, and she, although she had tried hard, had never managed more than a mild affection for her stepmother. Louisa dismissed the unhappy thought and got ready for bed. It was Thursday tomorrow, and Sir James had more patients than usual.

'I must take the car some time soon—' she had a little Fiat of her own '—and drive down to Stalbridge and see Aunt Martha.' She was a lady of great age, her father's elder sister. They seldom met but they liked each other. There would be no need to tell Felicity when she was going. Louisa put her head on the pillow with a contented sigh and went to sleep.

When she arrived at work the next morning Jilly was waiting for her. 'He's here,' she whispered. 'They were both here when I came. Asked for coffee, and there they were at the desk with books and papers all over the place.' She rolled her eyes. 'Planning something.'

Louisa, conscious of a thrill of interest at seeing Dr Gifford again, said, 'Jilly, you're letting your imagination run away with you again. They must have quite a bit of sorting out to do between them if Dr Gifford is to help out.'

Jilly gave her a pitying look. 'You're so sensible,' she observed. 'I don't know how...' She stopped as the door opened and Sir James poked his head round.

'Miss Howarth, will you come in, please? Jilly, when Mrs Grant arrives ask her to come here, will you?'

The sack? Was she to be made redundant? wondered Louisa, collecting pad and pencil and following Sir James. Was Dr Gifford full of ideas about running the practice, making more money? But heaven knew Sir James was doing very nicely. Surely Sir James wasn't going to retire...?

She gave Dr Gifford an austere good morning and, when bidden to sit, sat.

Sir James peered at her over his spectacles. 'I have received a wholly unexpected and urgent summons to the—ah—Middle East, Miss Howarth. It will necessitate my departure this afternoon. I may be gone for some time; at the moment I can say no more than that. Dr Gifford has most kindly agreed to take over as much of the practice as he can. Most fortunately he has a partner who is willing to co-operate fully.

'This will mean that your hours may be somewhat erratic, and Dr Gifford would be glad if you would be prepared to return with him to his own practice for those days when he is not here. In this way, everything can be kept up to date. It would mean your staying overnight once or twice a week. You have no objection?'

Louisa, not to be hurried, thought about it, and he went on quickly, 'Mrs Grant will come in each day as usual to take calls and so forth. You will have a good deal more work, but naturally you will be compensated for that.'

'Extra days off?' asked Louisa.

'Certainly. Or extra payment.'

'I'd rather have the days. Yes, of course, I'll help in any way I can, Sir James.'

The men exchanged a look. 'Splendid,' said Sir James, but Dr Gifford didn't say anything.

'Dr Gifford will take over from me at lunchtime

and there will be the normal consulting hours. We are fully booked for today, are we not?'

When she nodded, he added, 'Tomorrow's patients have already been notified; those in the morning will come as usual, the afternoon patients I have asked to come on the following day. As you are aware, I do not as a rule see patients at the weekend. But this leaves Dr Gifford free to return home tomorrow afternoon and return here late on Saturday morning.'

He paused. 'I make myself clear?' When she nodded again he added, 'You will be good enough to return with him tomorrow directly after the morning consulting hours, stay the night and return with the doctor ready for Saturday afternoon here. Sunday will be free.'

When Louisa said nothing he continued, 'Dr Gifford will come on Monday morning, stay until Tuesday noon, and then return to his own practice until Wednesday afternoon. You will go with him. There will be a good deal of work involved, reorganising the patients, but I believe that it can be done, especially when they realise that the circumstances are urgent and unusual.'

She longed to ask why, but she merely said, 'I will do all I can to be of assistance, Sir James.'

'Yes, yes, you're a good girl. I'm sure you will.' He looked up as there was a tap on the door and Mrs Grant came in. And the whole business was gone over again. If Mrs Grant was surprised she didn't allow it to show.

'Of course I'll do all I can to help, Sir James. I'm sure we'll manage until you get back.' She smiled at him and then at Dr Gifford, who smiled back at her— nicely too, Louisa noted. He hadn't said a word but she rather fancied that he had had a good part in the planning. Sir James was a brilliant man but liked someone else to dot his 'i's and cross his 't's. She gave a surreptitious glance at the desk and saw that the papers were maps of the Middle East and some airline ticket folders. She looked away, suddenly aware that Dr Gifford was watching her. He was going to be a hard taskmaster, she reflected.

Sir James asked suddenly, 'Miss Howarth, your stepmother will have no objection to your altered schedule?'

'I live on my own, sir.'

'Have I been told of your change of address?'

'Yes, sir; it's written in your address book on the desk and it was written into your day diary.'

He laughed. 'Can't catch you out, can I?'

'I should hope not, sir; I wouldn't be of much use to you if you could.'

He laughed again, in a high good humour. 'Well, that's settled, and thank you. I shall leave you and Dr Gifford to iron out any wrinkles.'

And there will be plenty of those, reflected Louisa. Not normally a gloomy girl, the immediate prospect didn't please her.

The first patients would be arriving very shortly, so she and Mrs Grant set about their various jobs, much hindered by Jilly's constant demands to be told what was happening.

'We'll tell you at lunchtime. Now, get on with your work, Jilly.' Mrs Grant sounded firm.

Patients came and went; the morning was busy. Louisa drank a cooled cup of coffee and wondered if she should tell Felicity. She decided not to; she would be away for one night only and that twice a week.

She hoped she would be welcome at the doctor's house.

She made a quick mental list of what she had better take in her overnight bag. Would she need her typewriter or computer? Surely he would have all that at his own practice? She supposed she would have to ask him. She dismissed these troublesome details from her head and picked up the phone; there were Sir James's clinics and ward rounds to sort out at the various hospitals he visited.

He left very shortly after the last patient had been seen. Dr Gifford had been with him for the entire morning and they came into the waiting room together. Sir James paused on his way out. 'I need hardly remind you to say nothing of my destination. I have your promise?'

They assured him of that willingly and wished him a good journey, and he said briskly, 'Well, I shall see you all again shortly. I'm sure you will do all you can to make things easy for Dr Gifford and our patients.'

The two men went then, and Louisa, nipping smartly to the window, watched them get into a discreet dark grey Bentley. Sir James drove a Rolls; this car must be Dr Gifford's. Oh, well, thought Louisa, at least I shall travel in comfort.

Jilly was all agog. 'I say, I wonder who he's going to see? Why is it all so hush-hush? I wish I knew...'

Mrs Grant said sternly, 'Jilly, you heard what Sir James said. Not a word to anyone. If you break your word he'll have you sacked. He could, you know, for leaking important information.'

'Really? You're not joking?' When Mrs Grant shook her head, Jilly said, 'I won't say a word—only

if he tells you about it when he comes back you will
tell me, won't you?'

'That's a promise. And if I don't know and Louisa
does, then she'll tell you, won't you, Louisa?'

'Cross my heart, I will. What time is the first patient coming? I wonder if Dr Gifford is coming back
before then? I've still got to get hold of Mrs Goulder
and ask her to come on Saturday morning. She won't
like that...'

Half an hour before the afternoon patients were due
to arrive, Dr Gifford came back. Louisa looked up as
he passed her desk.

'Will you bring your notebook with you, Miss
Howarth? We have ten minutes to spare, I believe.'

The look he gave her was indifferent, although his
voice was pleasant. She followed him into the consulting room and sat down, pencil poised.

'I should like to be sure that we fully understand
this rather complicated routine we must follow until
Sir James returns. I shall remain here until tomorrow
midday. You will accompany me back to my own
practice, stay the night so that we can work on the
patients for the following day, and return with me late
on Saturday morning. I must ask you to work during
Saturday afternoon, but you will be free on Sunday.'

Louisa said nothing; he was reiterating what she
already knew. He went on, 'I shall return here on
Monday morning, stay until noon on Tuesday and return to my practice until Wednesday afternoon. I believe there are two patients for the early evening?'
And, when she nodded, he added, 'I shall remain here
until Friday noon, when we will return to my practice.
We shall have the time then to sort out the patients

for the following week. And I will see Sir James's
patients on Saturday afternoon.'

There would be a lot of toing and froing, reflected
Louisa, and, of course, the only way he could cope
was to go over Sir James's patients' notes with her
whenever he could spare the time. Hopefully it would
only be for a short while. The whole thing had been
unexpected and there had been no time to make a
better arrangement.

She said, 'Very well, sir.'

He nodded without looking up from the papers on
the desk. 'Now, these patients this afternoon. Is there
anything special I should know about them?'

She replied promptly. 'Mrs Leggett will be here at
two o'clock. She's an old patient, but very nervous.
We usually give her a cup of tea after you've seen
her. Colonel Trump is next. Peppery, doesn't like to
waste time. Miss Fortesque is young and fashionable,
and likes to be buttered up.'

Dr Gifford's firm mouth twitched. 'You are most
helpful, Miss Howarth. I shall expect Mrs Grant here
as chaperon.'

'Well, yes,' said Louisa matter-of-factly. 'Sir James
always has her in for the ladies.' She added, 'It's not
quite the same as a general practice.'

She was treated to a cold stare from hard blue eyes.
'Thank you, Miss Howarth. I expect you wish to get
on with your work.'

Louisa snapped, 'Yes, I would. I'll let you have the
letters at the end of the afternoon.'

It surprised her when he got up and opened the door
for her, looking remotely over the top of her head as
he did so.

It wasn't until Mrs Leggett had come and gone and

Colonel Trump was closeted with the doctor that Louisa had the chance to speak to Mrs Grant. Jilly was in the little treatment room, setting it to rights, and for a moment they were alone.

'Will he do?' asked Mrs Grant. 'Mrs Leggett liked him.'

Louisa pulled a face. 'I dare say he's got a super bedside manner, only he isn't going to waste it on me. He looks through me, over me and round me, but hardly ever at me, and when he does it's like an icy draught. I don't think he likes me...'

'Nonsense, Louisa, everyone likes you. Shall you be able to manage with all the going back and forth? Is it really necessary?'

'I'm afraid it is. He's got to know something of Sir James's patients before he sees them as well as keeping an eye on his own practice. The idea is for us to get their notes sorted out between his surgery hours, so that by the time we get back here he'll have them all at his fingertips.'

'Poor man; he'll be worn out.'

'So shall I.'

'I dare say it won't be for long. Have we any idea how long Sir James will be away?'

'Not an inkling. I hope it's only for a few days.'

Miss Fortesque arrived then, in a cloud of expensive scent and wearing an artlessly simple outfit which must have cost the earth. She was wearing an armful of gold bangles which jingled and jangled, and she was in high spirits.

'I wasn't sure about coming; Sir James said that he was called away but that a colleague would see me. What's he like?'

'I'm sure you'll like him, Miss Fortesque,' said

Louisa, with just the right amount of enthusiasm in her voice. 'I'll show you in if you are quite ready.'

She opened the door, and Miss Fortesque swept past her and advanced with a little cry to where the doctor had risen to meet her. Louisa waited long enough to see him greet his patient with bland courtesy, but over that lady's head he shot Louisa a look which made her blink. 'If you would be good enough to send in Sister Grant?'

Miss Fortesque had been coming regularly for some months and she could never be hurried. Today the consultation lasted twice as long as usual, and when she finally came out of the consulting room she left in high spirits.

She tripped over to Louisa's desk and bent over it to whisper, 'He's gorgeous; I hope Sir James is away for a long time. Is he married?'

'I believe that he's engaged, Miss Fortesque. Sir James will be away only for a short time. Shall I book you in for your next appointment?'

'Yes, I'd better come sooner, I think. I don't feel as well. Next week, perhaps?'

'I'm afraid we're fully booked for the whole week. Shall I fit you in on the following week and let you know?'

'Yes, do that. Before Sir James gets back.' Miss Fortesque gave her a little smile. 'Lucky you, here all day with him. Though I don't suppose he really notices you.' Her gaze swept over Louisa's person, suitably dressed for her job with not a bracelet or earring in sight, and she smiled again.

Louisa got up. 'I'll show you out, Miss Fortesque,' she said, and ushered the lady through the door and closed it with a sigh of relief. She locked it, too. There were no more patients for the moment and they could have a cup of tea.

They had their tea sitting at her desk. Jilly had just carried Dr Gifford's tea tray in, and reported that he had thanked her nicely and smiled. 'He's on the phone,' she said. 'I like him.'

Mrs Grant chuckled. 'So did Miss Fortesque, but that cut no ice with him. Very professional, he was, lovely manners, beautiful bedside manner, too, but remote, if you know what I mean. I must say he's a remarkably handsome man.' She glanced at Louisa. 'He's good too; I'm not surprised Sir James got hold of him. Are they old friends, I wonder?'

'Perhaps you could find out when you go back with him tomorrow,' said Jilly.

'Certainly not,' said Mrs Grant. 'It's none of our business, Jilly. Let's get tidied up; old Lady Follett will be here very shortly.'

They were piling cups and saucers on the tray when the door opened and Dr Gifford put his head round. 'Miss Howarth, if you will come?'

He motioned her to a chair. 'Lady Follett. I see that Sir James intended to suggest hospital treatment. Does she know this?'

'No. He wrote to Mr Wolfitt, the surgeon he had in mind, and asked about beds and so on. We've had no reply as yet.'

He nodded. 'And Mr Tait—I see there's a query on his notes.'

'Mr Tait can't make up his mind whether to start a course of treatment or not.'

'Thank you.' He glanced up. 'You are most helpful, Miss Howarth.'

It was after six o'clock when Mr Tait left, still undecided, allowing them to clear up quickly and go home, leaving Dr Gifford sitting at his desk.

'Poor man,' said Mrs Grant as they wished each other goodnight on the pavement. 'I hope there's someone to look after him.'

'I should think he's quite capable of looking after himself,' said Louisa.

There were only two patients Friday morning, but both were new so they took a good deal longer than usual. Louisa, as neat as a new pin, her overnight bag safely in the cloakroom, got on with her work and wondered if there was any news of Sir James. She had seen Mrs Watts and explained that she would be away from her flat from time to time, and that lady had agreed to keep an eye on the place if she wasn't there.

'Mind you, I wouldn't do it for everyone, but, knowing it's the doctor that needs you to work for him, I'll do it willingly.'

Dr Gifford had said they would be leaving at noon and it was precisely that when he came into the waiting room. 'Ready?' he wanted to know, and added to Mrs Grant, 'You'll lock up and see to everything, Mrs Grant?' He gave her a charming smile. 'I've left my address and the phone number on the desk; don't hesitate to let me know if anything crops up which you can't deal with. You know what to say if anyone wants an appointment?'

'Yes, sir.'

He took Louisa's bag from her and ushered her out of the door and down to the pavement, wasted no time in urging her to get into his car, and drove away without speaking.

Louisa allowed five minutes to pass as he crossed the city. 'Where are we going?' she asked mildly.

'Gussage-up-Chettle, just this side of Cranborne.' He added, 'The practice is at Blandford; there are surgeries at Cranborne, Broad Chalke and Sixpenny Handley.'

'Very spread out,' said Louisa.

'There is a lot of rural country to cover. Normally we manage very well.'

'Well, let's hope that Sir James is back soon. Have you had any news of him?'

He was on the Blandford road, driving fast now. 'Yes.'

When he had nothing more to say, she said, 'All right, so you're not going to tell me anything. It's a good thing that this is a situation which will soon be over—I hope—for we don't get on, do we? Of course, it isn't your fault—you can't like everyone you meet, can you?'

He had turned off the main road and was driving quite slowly now along country lanes running between farm land. He said coldly, 'Far be it from me to dispute your opinion, Miss Howarth. Perhaps we might ignore our personal feelings and concentrate on what we have to do. I should appreciate your co-operation.'

'Oh, I'll co-operate,' said Louisa cheerfully. 'It wouldn't do for Sir James to come back to chaos, would it?'

His grunt told her nothing.

He turned a corner and there was Gussage-up-Chettle. A handful of cottages, a church set astride a crossroads, fields of ripening wheat stretching away towards gentle tree-covered hills.

'Oh, very nice,' said Louisa. 'I've never been here before.'

She didn't expect an answer and she didn't get one. He took the left-hand fork, turned in through an open gateway and stopped before a house half-hidden by trees and shrubs. Louisa got out and took a good look at it. It was what an estate agent would have described as a 'gentleman's residence', mostly Regency which had been added to from time to time, for it had a variety of windows at odd levels, wide eaves and a cluster of tall chimneys. The roof was tiled and its walls whitewashed, and the flowerbeds around it were stuffed with flowers—roses of every colour, scabias, wallflowers, morning glory, myrtle, late tulips, forget-me-nots; she lost count.

Dr Gifford had taken her bag from the boot. 'Come in; lunch will be ready.'

The door stood open, leading to a wide hall, its polished floor strewn with rugs. There was a console table under a giltwood Queen Anne mirror flanked by two side chairs, their high backs upholstered in green velvet. The walls were white with one or two fine paintings which she had no time to study, for the baize door at the back of the hall was opened and a woman as tall and big as Louisa came to meet them. She was middle-aged, her hair still dark, her features severe, but they broke into a smile as she reached them.

'Ah, there you are, Rosie,' said the doctor, and to Louisa, 'This is my housekeeper, Rosie, Miss Howarth. Rosie, will you take Miss Howarth up to her room?'

He turned to Louisa. 'Lunch in ten minutes. We shall have time to go through the post before my surgery.'

Louisa paused. 'What post?'

'I brought it with me from Salisbury. You can get it answered while you are here.'

He was walking away to a door at the side of the hall, and had it opened and went into the room beyond before she could utter a word.

'This way, miss,' said Rosie, and she led the way up a nice old oak staircase to the floor above. 'This will be your room, and if there's anything that you need you have only to say.'

Louisa stood in the doorway and looked around her. The room was charming and overlooked what appeared to be a very large garden at the back of the house. It was furnished simply but, she could see at a glance, there was every comfort there.

She said warmly, 'What a delightful room. Thank you, Rosie.'

The housekeeper nodded. 'Best not waste time; the doctor's a punctual man.'

She went away, leaving Louisa very tempted to waste ten minutes doing nothing. That wouldn't do, of course; she was here to work, and obviously the doctor had already arranged that to his satisfaction. She poked at her hair, did her face, took a quick, refreshing look out of the window and went downstairs.

Lunch was served in a large, airy room, its windows wide open. Its walls were panelled in a pale wood. There was a mahogany bow front sideboard, matching the Georgian dining table with its ring of matching dining chairs, and a carpet worn with age on the floor. A priceless carpet, Louisa thought, taking the chair the doctor had pulled back for her.

'Will you have some of this cold ham? One of the local farmers cures his own,' the doctor told her.

She accepted the ham and made a good lunch, for she saw no reason not to. Nothing was quite what she had expected but that couldn't be helped. The meal was delicious and she was hungry. Nevertheless she endeavoured to make conversation since that was the polite thing to do. But without much success. She was answered civilly, but it was obvious that the doctor was a man who never used two words if one would do.

They had their coffee at the table before he said abruptly, 'If you will come with me to my study, Miss Howarth?'

It was a comfortable room with an untidy desk, an old-fashioned mahogany office chair behind it and a couple of deep leather chairs drawn up on either side of the fireplace. Louisa sat down on one of the small chairs facing the desk and waited.

'I have been through most of the letters for Sir James,' said Dr Gifford, 'and made notes. If you would answer them suitably? Most of them are straightforward; most of them require two appointments. You have brought the appointment book with you? Arrange them as you think fit, using the timetable we have set up. Phone Mrs Grant if you need to, and any of the patients should you feel it necessary. Please make it clear that for the moment Sir James is away, and, if they prefer, give them a provisional date in ten days' time. We will deal with the reports from the path labs and hospitals this evening.'

'Where am I to work?'

'Here. I think you will find everything you will need. I hope to be back around five o'clock. Rosie will bring you tea. We will dine at eight and do the rest of the work this evening.'

He got up, saying to her surprise, 'Why not take a few minutes' stroll in the garden before you start? I'm going now; you won't be disturbed during the afternoon.' He turned at the door. 'Do you like dogs?'

'Yes.'

'I shall bring my dog back with me.'

He was holding the door open for her. As she went past him, she asked, 'What's his name?'

'Bellow.'

'Oh, that sounds like a Latin word—something to do with wars...'

He answered gravely, 'No, no, nothing so alarming. He has a permanent wheeze.'

'Oh, *bellow*, of course!' She smiled up at him and encountered his bland stare.

He opened a door at the back of the hall leading to the garden and left her then, and she went outside and strolled around, admiring everything. There was nothing formal about the garden, but it was beautifully tended and had been planned and planted by someone with a masterly eye. Just looking at it soothed her, although she wasn't sure why she needed to be soothed.

There was plenty of work for her to get on with during the afternoon. She dealt with the post in a competent manner, set aside anything she felt the doctor should see himself, and when a tray of tea came sat back and enjoyed it, feeling that she had earned it. And I only hope dinner will be a bit more sociable than lunch, thought Louisa, biting into the last of the scones.

It was tiresome to know so little about the doctor.

The practice was obviously a large and far-flung one; he had a partner and he must bear his share of the workload. But he was, after all, a GP, and unlike Sir James didn't have consulting rooms and a big private practice. She paused to think. She was only guessing; for all she knew he might be a brilliant medical man, preferring to hide his light under a bushel, coming out of obscurity in order to help Sir James.

'I really must find out,' said Louisa, talking to herself since there was no one else to talk to.

'What must you find out, Miss Howarth?' The doctor's voice, so quiet just behind her, took her by surprise so that she choked on her scone, coughing and spluttering while he thumped her back.

When she at last caught her breath, she said indignantly, 'What a beastly thing to do, creeping up on me like that...'

She turned round to look at him, standing there with a very large, silent dog at his side, and he said gravely, 'I do apologise. I had no idea that you were of a nervous disposition.'

Not an answer to soothe her already ruffled feelings.

CHAPTER THREE

LOUISA said, 'I am not in the least nervous, Dr Gifford.' And she held out a fist for Bellow to explore. 'This is Bellow? He looks magnificent. What breed is he?'

She spoke in the coldly polite voice of someone who had been brought up to be courteous at all costs, and the doctor hid a smile.

'His father was a St Bernard, his mother a Great Dane. A formidable parentage. Contrary to his appearance, he is a very mild dog, likes cats and children, but I have no doubt he would protect his own if they needed it.'

Louisa reflected that the doctor looked quite capable of protecting himself, but if Rosie was alone in the house Bellow would be splendid company.

Bellow sniffed at her fist and butted it gently with his great head.

Dr Gifford went to his desk and glanced through the orderly papers she had laid ready there. 'Finished? We have an hour or so before dinner...'

He sat down with Bellow beside him, and Louisa sat down opposite to him, and together they went through the work she had done and then worked their way through the list of Sir James's patients. It took quite a while.

He closed the diary finally. 'Shall we have drinks outside? It is a pleasant evening and we could both do with half an hour's peace.'

They sat in comfortable chairs under a mulberry tree at the end of the garden, drinking chilled white wine and making no attempt at conversation. When Rosie came to tell them that dinner would be in fifteen minutes, Louisa got up, murmured about tidying herself and went to her room. She was already quite tidy; she almost always was. She did her hair and face and deplored the fact that the only dress she had brought with her was the one she was wearing, a beautifully cut and expensive coat dress in stone-coloured shantung silk, entirely suitable for her job. And the epitome of good taste. All the same she would have liked to look more glamorous. Dr Gifford's complete uninterest in her person irked her.

He might have no interest in her but he was a good host. She was there under sufferance, as it were—certainly he would never have invited her—she was there to help out in a sudden and awkward situation.

And somehow, throughout dinner, he managed to remind her of that. Not that it mattered much. Louisa was hungry and Rosie was a splendid cook, providing watercress soup, rack of lamb and a magnificent toffee pudding. They maintained just sufficient conversation to be polite, had their coffee at the table and went back to the study to do more work. It was barely ten o'clock by the time the doctor was satisfied that everything was as near perfect as it could be.

'You must be tired,' he observed. 'I hope you have everything you need—Rosie will get anything you might want. Breakfast is at eight o'clock. I have a morning surgery before we leave.'

She bade him goodnight and went to her room. Someone had put a bowl of fruit and a bottle of water on the bedside table as well as the day's newspaper.

A well-run household, thought Louisa, lying in the bath, eating an apple. He might work hard, but there was no lack of comfort, luxury, even.

She slept soundly and went down to breakfast to find the doctor already at the table. He wished her good morning, hoped that she had slept well, and invited her to sit down and help herself.

He was sorting through his post as he spoke, and presently said, 'I shall be about two hours, if you will be ready to leave then? While I am gone perhaps you would sort out this lot for me—bills and so forth. My secretary at the surgery will deal with the rest.' He gave her a level look. 'It would be of great help to me.'

'Yes, of course, and phone calls?'

'If there are any. Put them through to the surgery if they are to do with patients—the number is on my desk. Anything social perhaps you can refuse—say I'm busy or going away.'

There were several phone calls, mostly of a social nature; it seemed that the doctor was both well known and well liked. Louisa, well versed in the art of graceful excuses, parried them all, made a note of them and drank the coffee Rosie brought her before going to get her overnight bag.

No time was wasted; the doctor came in on a surge of energy, picked up her bag, bade Rosie goodbye, bent to pull Bellow's ears with gentle affection and ushered Louisa into the car.

There was nothing to say for a time, until she told him of the morning's phone calls and reminded him that his first patient at Sir James's rooms was elderly and very deaf...

He nodded without speaking, and picked up the car

phone. 'Mrs Grant? We're on our way. Could you have coffee and sandwiches for us? Everything is all right?'

Apparently it was, and when they arrived Mrs Grant was waiting for them, coffee pot in hand.

A busy day, reflected Louisa, putting the key in her door that evening, and thank heaven that it was Sunday in the morning. They would start all over again on Monday morning, she supposed, and then go back to Gussage-up-Chettle, keeping one step ahead of the patients. She had rather enjoyed it.

There was no news of Sir James on Monday morning, and the week, an ordered muddle which strangely enough worked well, wore on. It was on Saturday, her final day of the week at the doctor's house, that Louisa made an interesting discovery.

She had been left to prepare the notes of the patients he was to see at Salisbury that afternoon and was closing the diary when she heard voices in the hall. The doctor and someone with him. The door of the study was half-open; she opened it a little wider and saw him standing there, and with him a girl. No, a woman, she corrected herself. An elegant creature, delicately made up, with ultra-golden hair, and wearing a silky patterned dress. Not suitable for the country, thought Louisa waspishly. She was fashionably thin, indeed not a curve was to be seen.

The doctor had seen her and it was too late to pretend that she hadn't seen them; Louisa went into the hall.

'Ah, Miss Howarth. Helena, this is Sir James's receptionist and secretary, who is helping me out for the moment.'

He glanced at Louisa. 'My fiancée, Helena Thornfold.'

Louisa was spared a brief glance before Miss Thornfold turned back to him.

'Darling, you can't go to Salisbury now I'm here. Cancel the patients or send Miss…to deal with them. I'm sure Sir James won't mind. It's ages since I saw you. Here's your housekeeper.' She ignored Rosie's greeting. 'Tell her to get lunch; I'm famished.' She gave his coat-sleeve a playful tug. 'You could go later.'

'I'm sorry, Helena, I have to go now. I'll drop you off on the way if you're staying with the Colliers. I hope to be back tomorrow; we'll see each other then.'

Miss Thornfold's mouth looked ugly; her large blue eyes narrowed. 'I shall probably have other plans.'

He said nothing, but spoke to Rosie, bade Bellow goodbye and picked up Louisa's bag. They went out to the car in silence broken only by Miss Thornfold's clear, high voice.

'I do so like your dress,' she told Louisa. 'Not everyone's style, of course, but you need to be careful, don't you? When you're big you have to wear clothes that don't call attention to your size.'

She smiled at Louisa and got in beside the doctor.

Louisa sat in the back and fumed silently, but after a while she found herself feeling sorry for the doctor. His Helena might be beautiful, but she would make him a terrible wife. She listened to Helena talking almost without pause, sometimes lowering her voice and tinkling with laughter. She was lavish with the 'darling's, too. Whether the doctor liked that or not it was hard to tell; he said almost nothing.

They were driving along different country roads; presumably the Colliers lived away from their usual route. Louisa glanced at her watch. There wasn't going to be much time to allow for delay unless Helena was dropped off very shortly. There would be no time for their coffee and Mrs Grant's quick up-dating.

The doctor turned sharply between high pillars, along a curved drive and stopped before the imposing entrance of a large house.

'Come in, just for a moment, darling,' cried Helena. 'A few minutes won't matter.'

Louisa couldn't hear what the doctor said but she saw him get out of the car, open Helena's door and say something again in a low voice. Helena glared at him and stalked away, and he turned back to the car.

'Get in front, please, Miss Howarth. There's still a small problem we must sort out before Monday morning.'

It was a warm summer's day and Louisa longed to be out of doors instead of sitting in the waiting room making polite conversation as the patients came and went again. There were forms to be posted, brief notes to type and a few phone calls to make before she could go home. Mrs Grant had left soon after the last patient; Louisa had made tea and taken a cup into the consulting room but the doctor had barely glanced up.

She had intended to go and see Felicity on Sunday—a brief visit after church—and then drive herself out of the city, away from the main roads. She would take a picnic...

She was ready to leave at last. She tapped on Dr

Gifford's door and poked her head round it. 'If there's nothing else, I'll go home. You'll be here on Monday morning?'

He glanced up. 'Yes.'

'Still no news of Sir James?'

'Not yet.'

'Let's hope it's soon. You're tired, aren't you?'

When he didn't answer, she added, 'She's all wrong for you, you know.' And at his look of outrage, 'There, I've let my tongue run away with me...'

He said, in a voice totally devoid of expression, 'Shall we consider that remark unsaid?'

She opened the door wider and came further into the room. 'That has always seemed to me such a silly thing to say. I mean to say, I've said it, so how can it be unsaid?' She gave him a wide smile for he looked tired. 'Don't let it worry you; I dare say something will happen to alter things.'

'What an abominable girl you are,' said Dr Gifford very quietly.

'You're annoyed. I'll go.' She closed the door quietly and left the surgery and he went to the window and watched her walk briskly away. Presently he started to laugh.

Louisa, cooking her supper, comfortable in a dressing gown and slippers, thought about him. Of course, she didn't like him, did she? But all the same she felt a vague concern for him. He was going to waste his life if he married Helena; she would hold him back from his work, which he undoubtedly loved, she would whine and moan and want things. And Rosie didn't like her; Louisa remembered the housekeeper's face when she had greeted Helena and been ignored.

Louisa tasted the kedgeree and decided it was just right, spooned it onto a warm plate and took it to the little table by the window. Her fork halfway to her mouth, she put it down again. 'Percy,' she said in a loud, satisfied voice. 'He's just right for her. Now, how can I get them to meet?'

Dr Gifford, unaware of the future being mapped out for him, drove himself home. He wasn't thinking about his patients, nor was he thinking about his future bride, he was thinking with a mixture of annoyance and amusement of Louisa.

His home was blissfully quiet when he reached it. Bellow came to meet him, and Rosie left him in peace for half an hour before serving him a splendid supper. Helena didn't phone; he hadn't expected her to for she had been resentful at not getting her own way and would probably sulk until he made amends. And he had so much more to think about.

So far, he had managed very well, and he had to admit that Louisa was a splendid help. An intelligent young woman, with good looks, she deserved a good husband. The doctor wasted some time deciding exactly what kind of man would be right for her and could not settle the matter to his satisfaction. Bellow put an end to his musing by demanding to go for a walk, and he dismissed her from his mind.

In the morning Helena phoned, her tantrum forgotten. He could come and fetch her, she told him, and invite her to lunch. 'There's so much we have to talk about,' she reminded him coaxingly.

So he spent his Sunday in her company and Helena was careful to be amusing and to ask all the right questions about his work, displaying an interest which was, in fact, completely lacking. She was well content to marry Thomas; he had money—and that to her was important—a pleasant lifestyle and a home she had every intention of refurbishing once they were married. That she didn't love him was unimportant; she would have everything she wanted. Besides, she had a wide circle of friends, and once she was his wife she would change his lifestyle. He could take on another partner; there was no need for him to spend so much time at his surgeries. He could let a junior partner take the calls from the more remote patients which took up so much of his time...

A young woman sure of her charm and good looks, she took it for granted that Thomas was in love with her. She had worked hard at getting him interested in her in the first place, but now he was safely hers she was becoming a little careless, allowing her selfishness and ill temper to show.

But today she was being careful, due to a slight unease at the thought of Louisa. Not at all Thomas's type, she told herself comfortably, but nonetheless someone of whom to be wary.

They had spent the afternoon in the garden, sitting under the mulberry tree, reading the Sunday papers. 'Like an old married couple,' she had said with a little laugh, and now, over the tea which Rosie had brought out to them, she said casually, 'You're lucky to have such a competent girl to help you while Sir James is away. I dare say she's clever?'

The doctor fed Bellow a biscuit. 'I've no idea. She understands her job and she's observant, which is a great help.'

'I found her quite lovely,' said Helena.

And when he didn't reply she asked, 'Do you admire that type? A lot of men go for it, all those curves...'

She glanced down complacently at her own front, with not a curve to be seen. 'So difficult to find clothes. Which reminds me, darling, I've bought the loveliest dress; you really must take me out so that I can wear it.'

'Of course. As soon as Sir James is back and I can get back to a normal life again.'

Helena laughed. 'What *you* call a normal life. I can see that when we are married I shall have to change all that.'

To which he said nothing. He looked placid and pleasantly relaxed, sitting there beside her, and it didn't enter her head to wonder what he was thinking.

Louisa got up early on Monday morning, ate a splendid breakfast, dressed in another of her unassuming outfits, this time a smoky blue dress with a white collar and cuffs, and went to work. Dr Gifford wouldn't be there until just before ten o'clock, when the first patient would arrive, but she had no doubt that there would be plenty of work for her to get on with.

Mrs Grant hadn't arrived yet, nor had Jilly, so she opened windows and drew back curtains, put the kettle on and went into the consulting room.

Dr Gifford was at the desk, writing. He looked up as she went in, wished her good morning, and added, 'Sir James will be returning late this evening. He suggests that he takes over on Wednesday morning and that we should deal with everything until then. I'll stay until this evening and return here tomorrow morning. There is no need for you to come to

Gussage-up-Chettle; I'll stay late and look out the notes.'

Louisa said, 'Very well, Dr Gifford,' and wondered why she had this sudden sense of disappointment. Wasn't it something she had been hoping for ever since Sir James had gone away? She would miss the lovely old house and Bellow and Rosie's kindness, and to be honest she was going to miss Dr Gifford...

There was no time to say more and, in any case, it seemed that nothing more was going to be said.

Mrs Grant, apprised of the news, expressed satisfaction, and Jilly, when she was told, said mournfully, 'We shan't see him again; it will be so dull when he's gone.'

'You'll be too busy to be dull, my girl,' said Mrs Grant bracingly. Unusually for a Monday, there were more patients than usual, and several of those came late, so that Louisa was kept busy offering soothing cups of tea and coffee to those who had perforce to wait their turn. It meant that their lunch hour was curtailed, while the doctor made do with coffee and biscuits before fitting in a visit to a hospital where one of his patients had been admitted. And the afternoon was just as bad.

Mrs Grant, clearing up with swift efficiency, sent Jilly home and prepared to leave herself.

'You're coming?' she asked Louisa.

'Well, I hope so. I'll wait a bit in case there are any letters or appointments to make.'

She began to clear her own desk, but when the doctor opened his door and asked her to go in she picked up her notebook and pencil and went to sit by his desk.

He had the appointment book open before him; tomorrow was as full as that day had been. 'Could we run through these notes quickly? I shall be here all day but there won't be time to check them tomorrow.'

'But you're going home this evening?'

'Yes. I'll be as quick as I can; it's been a long day.'

All the same it was a good hour later when he declared himself satisfied. He said stiffly, 'I'm sorry to have kept you, Miss Howarth. I'll see you in the morning.'

Louisa closed her notebook. 'Did you have any lunch?'

He gave her a look of faint surprise. 'No.'

'And only a cup of coffee... Are you hungry?'

He smiled then. 'Indeed I am, but I must get back; there is a patient of mine at Cranborne I must see before I go home.'

'In that case,' said Louisa, 'you'd better come back to my flat and have a sandwich to keep you going. It'll only take ten minutes or so and you'll feel all the better for it.'

He looked at her thoughtfully and then surprised her by saying, 'Thank you, I would like that. If it's not too much trouble?'

'Well, I have to eat, too,' said Louisa matter-of-factly.

The drive to her flat took only a couple of minutes. She unlocked her door and led the way upstairs and into her little sitting room.

'Sit down; I'll be a few minutes.'

She left him there, in her little easy chair which was too small for him, and went into the kitchen.

Her cupboards were well stocked; she made ham sandwiches and coffee, and took them into the sitting room. The doctor was wandering round the room looking at the water colours she had hung on the walls. He sat down at her nod, observing, 'Those are charming paintings.'

'Yes, aren't they? My home until Mother died. A family friend did them and Father gave them to me. Do sit down and eat something. It's only sandwiches and coffee, but there's plenty of both.'

She watched him demolish the sandwiches; he must have been famished. She nibbled slowly so that he could have the lion's share and fetched more coffee.

They didn't talk much; the next day's patients had been dealt with, so for the moment they were free of their work. Louisa, casting about her for a suitable topic of conversation, asked, 'Will you be going to the Woodleys' ball? I'm sure Miss Thornfold must know them. Megan—the youngest daughter, you know—has got engaged, so it's to be an especially brilliant affair.'

She glanced up at him and saw his thoughtful look, and blushed. Of course, he would think that she was fishing for details of his private life...

The doctor watched the blush, knowing quite well why it had appeared. It looked charming; his Helena had, as far as he could remember, never blushed. He said casually, 'Yes, we shall be there. You will be going? They know almost everyone within miles around, don't they?'

Louisa handed him more sandwiches. 'Yes, I went to school with Cissie, the eldest girl, and Father knew them well.'

He finished the sandwich and put down his mug. 'You have been most kind.' He sounded remote; perhaps he had just remembered Helena. 'I feel a new man.'

He got up, and she got up with him, wished him a brisk goodnight, let him out of the flat and then went to the window and watched him drive away. He didn't look up.

She was still hungry, of course; one ham sandwich wasn't very filling. She went into the kitchen, cleared away the plates and mugs, made herself scrambled eggs on toast and poured herself a glass of white wine. She was halfway through her meal when she gave a little whoop of satisfaction.

The Woodleys' ball. He was going with the horrid Helena, and Percy would be there. What a chance to engineer their meeting and get her off the doctor's back. She didn't pause to wonder if he would like that to happen, but began to think of ways and means.

A pity that she had parted from Percy in a less than friendly manner. He was a conceited man, though. If she could contrive to charm him into going with her as her partner that would make her plans easier. A new dress, of course, and a wistful manner, and the diamond earrings to remind him of what he might have had...

The doctor, looking even more remote than usual, arrived punctually the next day. He was, as always, immaculately turned out, and he had the look of a man who had had a good night's sleep. Louisa, as usual uttering her thoughts before making sure that they were suitable to utter, bade him a good morning and asked if he had had a pleasant evening with Miss Thornfold.

The look he gave her would have shattered a lesser mortal, but Louisa was made of sterner stuff. 'All work and no play,' she reminded him, and gave him a sunny smile.

It was another busy day, and at the end of it there were the last-minute arrangements to make. Sir James, presumably, would be at his desk at his usual hour in the morning.

'Will you be here?' asked Louisa, arranging the diary and calendar just so on Sir James's desk.

The doctor glanced up briefly. 'Yes, Miss Howarth.' That was all he had to say until they were getting ready to leave, when he thanked them all for their help before going back to his desk.

The three of them stood on the pavement, exchanging end-of-the-day gossip before going their various ways.

'He'll be glad to get back to his own surgery,' said Mrs. Grant. 'You'll miss your trips to Gussage-up-Chettle, won't you, Louisa?'

'Yes, it made a nice change. I suppose that if he's going to help Sir James from time to time we shall see him occasionally. But there won't be any need for me to go there again.'

Something she deeply regretted.

Sir James arrived at his usual time in the morning. He looked tired, tanned by the sun and a trifle self-important. But it seemed he could be forgiven that for he had successfully dealt with what might have been a mortal illness for a VIP in the Middle East, a man who had the potential to upset the whole delicate balance of power there. He said very little of this, though. It wasn't until their lunch hour that Jilly went out to get their sandwiches and returned with a variety of newspapers full of it.

Sir James had dealt with his patients in a perfectly normal way, and when later in the morning Dr Gifford arrived they had spent a long time in the consulting room and then gone out to lunch together. It wasn't until the end of the day that he came into the waiting room and thanked them for carrying on in his absence.

'I much appreciate it,' he told them. 'And Dr Gifford tells me that you have all been most helpful, especially you, Miss Howarth. Your days have been sadly upset; the least I can do is offer you a day off.' He added prudently, 'It seems that Friday will be a fairly quiet day; perhaps you would like that?'

Louisa thanked him nicely. She would like it very much; she would go up to London and look for a dress...

No one had said anything about Dr Gifford coming in. He stood by calmly, saying nothing at all. It was Sir James who told them that his colleague would be coming in twice a week as originally planned. 'But not for the rest of this week,' he added. 'I'm afraid his own practice has been sadly disrupted and he will need a few days to get it back into some sort of order.'

Louisa decided against going to see Felicity until the weekend. It was very likely that she would see Percy there then, and she was anxious to carry out her plan for the ball. She had bidden Dr Gifford goodbye and sent her love to Bellow and, since everyone else had been there when she'd done so, she had kept her voice impersonal.

His laconic 'My thanks for your help, Miss Howarth,' couldn't have been more casual.

He didn't deserve the trouble she was taking over him, she reflected, but he would live to thank her...

*   *   *

She took her time buying the dress. She could afford to make a careful choice—something special, something which would catch Percy's eye and, she hoped, the doctor's. She searched patiently, knowing what she wanted, and she found it at length. A pale apricot crêpe over a satin slip, its colour complementing her hair. It was a very simply cut dress and it was a perfect fit.

She took it home and tried it on, examining as much of her person as possible in the narrow mirror inside the wardrobe door. She would need evening shoes and, since it was high summer and she would drive herself or be driven by Percy, she could wear her gossamer lacy wool wrap. Well satisfied, she went to bed and slept the sleep of someone who had achieved a praiseworthy purpose.

She waited until teatime on Sunday before going to see Felicity and, as she had hoped, Percy was there. There were a number of other people there, too, so she made her way round the room, keeping well away from him. A strategy which worked, for presently she found him beside her.

'Avoiding me, Louisa?' He sounded smug. 'You have no need to; I bear you no grudge.' He gave her a sly look. 'Having second thoughts, my dear? A woman may always change her mind, you know.'

Louisa toyed with a cucumber sandwich. 'Well, no, not exactly, but we ought to stay friends, oughtn't we, Percy? We've known each other for such a long time.'

'Then we must try and see more of each other, mustn't we? It would please Felicity.'

Louisa looked down modestly at her feet, which were clad in elegant Italian shoes. Of course it would please Felicity; Percy was one of the richer fish swimming in the sea... 'It would be nice, only I'm so busy. I'd hoped I might be able to go to the Woodleys' Ball...'

'Of course you are going; you don't need to work in the evenings, do you?'

'No, of course not.' She had a sudden memory of sitting in Dr Gifford's study, working on patients' notes. 'But I dare say I shall be too tired. Besides, I don't like going on my own...'

Her voice was just sufficiently wistful.

'My dear girl, you'll come with me. I'll pick you up with the car; you won't need to do anything but get dressed.' He added in a self-righteous voice, 'For the sake of our long-standing friendship, Louisa, and in the hope you will find that an evening together will lead to a better understanding between us.'

Only Percy could be as pompous as that. She said meekly, 'Oh, Percy, that's awfully kind of you. It's next Saturday, isn't it?'

'Yes. We don't need to get there until it's well started. I'll call for you around eight o'clock; it'll take half an hour to drive there.' He put a hand on her arm. 'Supposing we meet one evening...?'

She was saved from answering by Felicity. 'You two have been talking long enough,' she said peevishly. 'I can't think what you have to say to each other. Louisa, do go and talk to Colonel Lauder; he's so deaf.'

Louisa made her escape presently, unnoticed by anyone in the room. She went to see Biddy, sharing a cup of strong tea with her while the old lady gossiped. Mrs Howarth was leading a very active social life, she assured Louisa, out most evenings and people to lunch and dinner.

'Have you had your wages?' asked Louisa.

'Well, as to that, Miss Louisa, I dare say the missus has forgot...'

Louisa opened her purse. 'Supposing I pay you now? I can get the money back from Mrs Howarth easily enough.'

She uttered the fib cheerfully and presently went back to her flat. Her plan was working. Of course, she would have to deal with Percy later, but that was something she wasn't going to bother about at the moment.

The days settled down into their normal routine once more, and Dr Gifford came in twice the following week. An unused room on the same floor had been furnished for him and his name was on the door, but Louisa saw very little of him. True, she got out his patients' notes for him, took his messages and phone calls and made his appointments, but, beyond a civil greeting and any necessary requests he might make, he had nothing to say to her.

A different man from the one who had devoured ham sandwiches in her flat, reflected Louisa. Perhaps he had quarrelled with his Helena. That might account for the faint frown and the cold blue eyes. Ah, well, thought Louisa, we'll see what happens at the ball.

The day of the ball dawned bright and warm, ideal for the event, for the Woodleys owned a lovely country house with vast grounds and guests would be able to stroll around between the dancing. Louisa spent the afternoon washing her hair, doing her nails and examining her face for spots.

The Woodleys would be sure to have a marvellous display of food, but that would be later in the evening. She prudently boiled an egg and made a pot of tea before starting to dress.

The dress was everything she had hoped for, and the shoes, slender straps supporting a high heel which would add several inches to her height, matched exactly. She piled her hair in her usual fashion, hooked in the earrings and took careful stock of her face. She wanted to look her best—not for Percy, but certainly for Helena. She ignored the thought that she wanted to look nice for Dr Gifford.

Percy came punctually, suggesting that they might sit for half an hour over a glass of wine before they left.

'And it would be just your luck to be stopped and breathalysed,' Louisa pointed out. 'We can have all the wine we want when we get there.'

'You look gorgeous,' said Percy, his eyes on the earrings.

He would have kissed her then, but she was too quick for him and led the way down to the car. Once there she asked one or two leading questions about his work, so that he carried on a monologue for the whole of their journey.

Once at their destination, she promised to meet him in the main hall and went upstairs to Cissie's bedroom to dispose of her wrap and take a careful look at her person. Cissie came in while she was there.

'Louisa, how lovely to see you, and don't you look gorgeous? Who've you come with?'

'Percy.'

Cissie looked surprised. 'But I thought you'd managed to get rid of him for good...'

'Well, I have. Only I need him this evening for a reason.'

'You've got your eye on another man…'

'Not really. I want Percy to meet someone—a girl. Perhaps you know her? Helena Thornfold.'

'Her? That stick! She's going to marry Thomas Gifford; do you know him?'

'Yes.'

Cissie chuckled. 'Percy and Helena; they're just right for each other.'

'That's what I thought,' said Louisa. 'Shall we go down?'

CHAPTER FOUR

PERCY was waiting. He said impatiently, 'You've been a long time; what kept you? I've been standing here...'

'I was talking to Cissie. Shall we go and find the Woodleys?'

The place was crowded and, once they had exchanged greetings with their host and hostess, they worked their way slowly through the rooms until they reached the ballroom built onto the back of the house. That was crowded, too, and it took Louisa a minute or two to see Felicity, exquisitely gowned, dancing with a portly man with a drooping moustache.

'Who's he?' asked Louisa.

Percy shrugged. 'New here. Bought that converted barn near Broadchalke; spent thousands on it, I hear. He fancies Felicity.' He added with a faint sneer, 'He's wealthy.'

They joined the dancers then, and Louisa, listening with half an ear to Percy, scanned the crowded room. There was no sign of Dr Gifford or Helena. Perhaps he had been prevented at the last moment; perhaps they had decided that they would rather spend the evening together... Louisa felt a quite unexpected pang at the thought.

'You aren't paying attention,' said Percy. 'Did you hear what I said?'

'No—sorry. This is fun, isn't it?'

'I fail to see what fun there is in a private ball,'

said Percy pompously. 'I was suggesting that we might spend Sunday together.'

'Why?'

'So that we may resume our relationship, Louisa.'

'But we never had one and I don't want to.'

If the doctor and Helena didn't turn up the whole evening would have been wasted, for Percy was going to cling... She saw them then, the doctor towering head and shoulders above those around him, head bent slightly to listen to Helena—a magnificently gowned Helena, silver sequins on a jade-green silk shift, cut far too low over her regrettable lack of bosom. She was wearing far too much jewellery.

When the music stopped Louisa edged Percy towards the other end of the room, where she could see the other two. She made her way towards them unhurriedly, aware that she looked nice and hoping that the doctor thought so, too. He had seen her, of course, and returned her greeting with a faint smile. Helena smiled too, while she surveyed Louisa's person with a cold eye.

She said now, 'Oh, hello; you managed to find something to wear,' and then bit her lip for, of course, the two men looked at Louisa.

Louisa gave them her sunny smile. 'Do you know Percy Witherspoon? I dare say you will have heard of him; his family have been lawyers since one of his ancestors donated money towards building the cathedral. Percy, this is Helena Thornfold, Dr Gifford's fiancée.'

The two of them shook hands and Percy, Louisa noticed with satisfaction, held Helena's a little too long. She certainly was dazzlingly pretty, even if overdressed. And she had looked at Percy with inter-

est. Louisa thought that Helena might be a snob, and
Percy, whatever his shortcomings, bore a respected
and ancient name. She gave a very small sigh of satisfaction and looked up to see the doctor's eyes on
her.

He said most politely, 'Do you care to dance, Miss
Howarth?' and whisked her onto the floor and danced
her off to the other end of the room.

He said gently, 'I ask myself why, Miss Howarth.'

She had to look up to him; it was a nice change
from the crown of Percy's slightly balding head. 'I
can't think what you mean, Dr Gifford.'

'Let us not beat about the bush. Why were you so
anxious that Helena and Witherspoon should meet?
And why are you so pleased about it? What scheme
are you hatching?'

'Me? Hatch a scheme?' Louisa was all wide-eyed
innocence. 'I wouldn't know how! I saw you across
the floor and I thought it would be nice for Percy to
meet your Helena. She is really very beautiful, you
know.'

'Yes. I do know. Let us hope Percy is as pleased
at the meeting as you appear to be. He is yours, I
presume?'

'Percy? Good heavens, no. We've known each
other for ever.' She added artlessly, 'He doesn't really
want to marry me, you know. It would be convenient,
I suppose. I mean, it would save him having to look
around for a wife, and I'm suitable. Besides, I've
money of my own which, as a lawyer, he finds an
added bonus.'

The doctor received this information with a straight
face. 'I hope Percy doesn't think that I might free
Helena if he should consider her as a future wife.'

'No, no. I'm sure he doesn't.'

They were dancing with easy skill, her steps matching his without effort.

Louisa took another look at his face. 'When?' she asked.

'I believe it is the bride's privilege to name the day.'

'Snubbed,' said Louisa. 'How's Bellow?'

'In excellent health, and Rosie asked me to give you her love if I saw you.'

'Did she? Did she really? She's a dear, isn't she? And a marvellous cook. You're awfully lucky, having her for a housekeeper to look after you.' And added as an afterthought, 'And Helena, of course.'

'Of course,' said Dr Gifford.

Percy and Helena were dancing together. Percy was talking and Helena was listening with every appearance of interest. Louisa couldn't resist remarking on how well they suited each other.

'In what way?' asked the doctor blandly. He was looking over the top of her head and she knew that he was angry. Oh, well, she had cooked her goose, hadn't she? He would dislike her even more than before, and whatever had possessed her in the first place? It really didn't matter what she said.

'They're alike, aren't they? I mean, they like talking about themselves.' She went on thoughtfully, 'Mind you, that's only my opinion, and if I were as beautiful as Helena I'd talk about myself, too. She should be a fashion model...'

'A generous remark since you give me the opinion that you don't like Helena.'

'Not generous, it's the truth; she's quite lovely. But you don't need me to tell you that. You must be very proud of her.' She glanced up at him and met a cold stare.

'You must forgive me if I decline to discuss my private life with you, Miss Howarth.'

'Oh, that's all right,' said Louisa cheerfully. 'We're not likely to see much of each other, are we? When you come to the consulting rooms I don't expect you to say more than ''Good morning'' and ''Good evening, Miss Howarth''.'

The music stopped and she said, 'There, now you can take me back to Percy and forget me.'

The doctor looked at her. He would take her back to Percy, since that was what was expected of him, but he wouldn't forget her. How could he? Standing there in her lovely, simple gown, her glorious hair very slightly untidy, saying just what came into her head with no thought of the results.

They started to cross the room, an unhurried process since they both knew so many of the people there, and, before they could reach Percy and Helena, Felicity joined them.

'Darling, there you are. Isn't this fun…?'

She looked at the doctor and Louisa said, 'Hello, Felicity. Do you know Dr Gifford? Doctor, this is my stepmother, Mrs Howarth.'

Felicity could be very charming. She touched the doctor's sleeve lightly. 'We've never met, but I know the name. The Thornfolds are friends of mine, and you're to marry Helena, are you not? I saw her just now—she's with Percy Witherspoon.' She looked at Louisa. 'I thought he came with you, darling?'

'He did. I'm on my way back to him.'

'Oh, darling, if only you meant that—he's still so upset.' And at Louisa's frown she added, 'I'll not say another word.' The music struck up again and she said, 'Oh, I'm longing to dance again,' and smiled up at Dr Gifford.

The doctor had beautiful manners. 'I should be delighted.' He glanced at Louisa. 'You will excuse us?'

He didn't wait for her answer, but she hadn't expected him to. She wasn't surprised to see Percy and Helena dancing together. They danced very correctly, talking earnestly. Louisa wondered uneasily if Dr Gifford would mind—perhaps he really was in love with Helena? There had never been any sign of his feelings, and Helena, she felt sure, wasn't a woman to welcome any kind of display of affection in public. Perhaps he was one of those in whom feelings ran deep...

She was swept away to dance with one of the Woodley boys, and after him there was a succession of partners. From time to time she glimpsed Dr Gifford with a variety of partners and occasionally Helena. She found herself dancing with Percy once more, and as he guided her with stiff correctness round the floor she listened to his comments upon Helena.

'A delightful creature, and we have so much in common and agree about so much that is wrong in this decade.'

'Oh?' said Louisa, and prepared herself for a prosy sermon about no smoking, no drinking, money in the bank and the satisfaction of running an economical household. She didn't say so, but she did wonder if Helena actually lived up to these high-sounding notions. It seemed unlikely.

But supposing Helena did? Remembering her own visits to the doctor's house, Louisa reflected that even though he worked hard his household was run on very comfortable lines—there had been no cheeseparing there. There had been no ostentatious display of wealth either, but she had no doubt that he maintained a lifestyle far removed from the one that Percy was lecturing her about.

Louisa said, 'Oh, indeed, yes,' in an interested voice, and lost herself in thought. Supposing that were so? Would Helena insist on changing everything? Dr Gifford would put up with that if he loved her, but it would change him. Louisa suddenly wanted him to stay as he was—tiresome and terse and aloof, but nonetheless happy in his home.

'And there's Bellow and Rosie,' said Louisa, speaking her thoughts out loud.

Percy paused in his measured summing up. 'What did you say? I don't care to be interrupted.'

Louisa murmured, and Percy cleared his throat preparatory to resuming his monologue, but fortunately the music stopped and Louisa said quickly, 'Oh, look, Felicity is beckoning. I'd better go…'

Halfway across the room she was halted by Dr Gifford. The hand on her arm was urgent. 'One of the guests has been taken ill; Mrs Woodley has asked me to see her. Will you come with me?' He smiled a little. 'You're a sensible woman and will do whatever I ask you to without fuss.'

'Thanks a lot,' said Louisa. 'Yes, of course I'll come. Aren't there any nurses here?'

'No, if there had been I wouldn't have troubled you. And no one is to be told.'

He walked her unhurriedly to one of the doors and strolled through with her in tow. 'Upstairs,' he said then, and urged her across the hall and up the great curved staircase.

Mrs Woodley was waiting for them in the gallery above. 'In here,' she told them as she glanced at Louisa. 'Oh, good. You're so sensible, Louisa.'

Twice in five minutes, thought Louisa. I wonder what they would think if I should faint gracefully all over the patient?

The girl lying on the bed was pale and frightened, and the young man holding her hand was even paler. Dr Gifford paused to look at them and took charge of the situation with calm ease.

'It's the baby,' said the husband. 'We've been dancing...'

Dr Gifford said kindly, 'How many months? Pain? Uncomfortable? When did this start?'

'About fifteen minutes ago.'

'Then I'll take a look, shall I?' He looked at Mrs Woodley. 'I expect you want to get back to your guests. I'll just make sure that everything is all right, and, if necessary, Louisa will let you know what's happening.'

Mrs Woodley nodded and went away, and the doctor said cheerfully, 'Now, Mr... I don't know your name...'

'Davidson.'

The doctor laid a large, comforting hand on the young man's shoulder. 'I'd like you to go to another room for a while. Miss Howarth will stay here and be with your wife while I examine her. It won't take long.'

Mr Davidson kissed his wife and went, and the doctor said in a soothing voice, 'Now, Mrs Davidson, I'm going to make sure that everything is all right. It won't hurt, and Miss Howarth will hold your hand. Have you felt any discomfort before this evening?'

He was quick and gentle and calmly sure of himself. Presently he said, 'Everything seems quite all right. All the same, I think that the best thing would be for you to go home and go to bed. Tell me the name of your doctor and I'll let him know what happened and ask him to visit you. Where do you live?'

'Tollard Royal; we came with the Jefferies.' Mrs. Davidson tugged at Louisa's hand. 'We can't ask them to leave, it's still early.' She had a small, very young face and she had been crying.

Louisa said bracingly, 'Don't worry, Dr Gifford will think of something.'

He was washing at the basin in the corner of the room. He dried his hands, rolled down his shirtsleeves and got back into his jacket before saying easily, 'I'll drive you and your husband back, Mrs Davidson. Miss Howarth will come with us to keep you company. Shall we let him know?'

The two men talked for a minute or two, then the doctor asked, 'Does anyone know if there is a back staircase? I'll get the car and have it at a side entrance. Stay just as you are; I'll carry you down when I come back. Louisa, come with me and find the back stairs, and get your wrap. When you get back here, perhaps Mr Davidson will find your friends. Explain that your wife has developed a shocking headache and you're taking her home, that you have a car—say you borrowed it—make some excuse. Then come back here as soon as you can, and bring your wife's wrap with you.'

He caught Louisa's hand and urged her out of the

room. 'You're a friend of the family. Which is the quickest way out?'

She knew the house well. A wide corridor branched into two passages, and at the end of one were the back stairs.

'Good girl. Now, off you go and be quick about it.'

He disappeared down the stairs and she went to find her wrap and go back to Mrs Davidson, who was in tears again. Louisa cuddled her in her arms and murmured soothingly. 'Don't worry; I'm sure everything will be all right. I believe it's quite usual to have these scares, and you're young and strong, aren't you?'

She was mopping Mrs Davidson's unhappy face when first her husband and then the doctor returned. 'You told Mrs Woodley?' he asked Louisa.

She nodded. 'I said you'd let her know.'

He grunted, picked up Mrs Davidson and carried her down the stairs, through a damp, dark passage and out of a side door leading to a deserted courtyard.

'Get in the back,' he told Louisa, and when she did so he settled his patient carefully beside her. 'Put your arms around her and hold her steady.' He turned to Mr Davidson. 'Get in, there's a good chap. I've got hold of your doctor; he should be at your place by the time we get there.'

As the crow flew the Davidsons didn't live all that far away—but the country lanes took no heed of a crow; they wound their own, wandering ways and didn't encourage speed. Louisa, holding Mrs Davidson close, was relieved when the doctor stopped outside a thatched house standing well back from the road in a large garden.

Louisa, sent ahead to turn down the bed, blundered

around looking for light switches and pulling curtains. How like a man, she reflected crossly, sending her upstairs in a strange house and expecting everything to be just so within seconds. Mr Davidson hadn't been of much help either; he had rushed to the phone, intent on making sure that the doctor understood the urgency of the case. Dr Gifford, quite unflurried, bore his patient upstairs, laid her gently on the bed, and suggested in a voice which expected no denial that Louisa should undress Mrs Davidson and call him the moment it was done.

Mrs Davidson was weeping again. Louisa, helping her out of her—fortunately—few clothes, kept up a steady flow of chat. 'And I can't go on calling you Mrs Davidson. My name's Louisa…'

'Mary—and my husband's Ricky. I'm so grateful to you and Thomas—he told me to call him Thomas; he's a dear, isn't he? Everyone likes him.' Mary, distracted for a minute from her own woes, added, 'Such a pity he's got engaged to that Thornfold girl—' She broke off at the sound of voices, and a moment later all three men came into the room.

Dr Gifford didn't stay, though; he waited long enough for Ricky to say something cheerful to his wife and led him away. 'You'll stay, of course,' he said to Louisa as they went.

The Davidsons' doctor was elderly, with a lovely, soothing bedside manner, and Mary, reassured as to her well-being, cheered up.

'I guessed that you might be feeling a little nervous at being alone with only your husband.' He glanced at Louisa. 'Your friend and Dr Gifford will want to return to their party, so I phoned an excellent nurse who takes private cases; she should be here within half an hour or so. She will stay for a day or two until you feel quite yourself again and she will report to me.'

He went away presently, and Louisa sat Mary up against her pillows. 'You'd like me to wait until the nurse comes?'

'Oh, would you? Ricky is a darling, but he wouldn't know what to do. I'm sure she won't be long.'

'Shall I go and make a cup of tea while we're waiting?'

'Would you? Ricky may have done that.' She sounded doubtful. 'We have a housekeeper but she doesn't sleep here.'

Her husband came then, and Louisa went down to the kitchen, a cosy place, splendidly equipped. The two doctors were in the room across the hall, and she could hear the murmur of their voices. She put the kettle on and poked her head round the door.

'Tea? Or there's coffee.'

They turned to look at her, blandly polite in their refusal. She shouldn't have disturbed them. When eggheads got together they didn't need mundane things like cups of tea. She bore a tray upstairs and found the Davidsons holding hands. This was no place for her either; she made a quick excuse about seeing to the doctors and went downstairs again with her own mug. She drank her tea in the kitchen, feeling rather hard done by.

She was tidying things away when the nurse arrived. After five minutes with the doctors, she took over with a friendly competence and lack of fuss. She had gone straight to her patient, but presently she came into the kitchen.

'Joan Wright. I hear you've been everyone's right hand. A good thing that Dr Gifford and you were on hand. He's one of those reliable men who always turns up when he's wanted.'

'Oh, you know him?'

'Goodness me, yes. Worked for him on and off for years. I'm to tell you that he's ready to leave; he thought you might want to say goodbye to Mrs Davidson first.'

'Yes, yes, of course. But isn't there anything I can do for you? Make up a bed or get a tray ready for you?'

'Bless you for the thought. There's a small guest room with the bed made up, and I had supper only a couple of hours ago. I shall creep down in the small hours and boil an egg.'

'Will Mrs Davidson be all right?'

'So far there's no damage. If she stays quiet for a day or two we shall soon know.' She smiled. 'You must be longing to get back to the ball.'

Louisa said, 'Yes,' rather uncertainly. Excuses and explanations would have to be made to Percy and Felicity, not to mention Helena, although that would be Dr Gifford's lot. She didn't envy him!

The Davidsons were too self-absorbed to do more than utter vague thanks and goodnight, and she couldn't blame them. She found her wrap and went down to the hall and found the two doctors standing at the open door.

'There you are,' said Dr Gifford in a voice which suggested that she had kept him waiting for a long time. She gave him a cross look, shook hands with his colleague, and presently they got into the car.

Let him be the first one to speak, she reflected; a

few graceful words of thanks and an apology for spoiling her evening wouldn't go amiss.

'Are you hungry?' It was so unexpected that she turned to look at him. He turned his head briefly and smiled. 'I'm famished.'

'Yes, so am I.' It was difficult to speak coldly with her head filled with the prospect of a meal. There didn't seem to be any more to say so she kept silent, watching the narrow, dark road ahead of them. Presently she said, 'We didn't come this way.'

'No. We'll go to my place and have a quick meal before we go back to the Woodleys'.'

'But it's just past midnight...'

'I think it likely that the ball will go on well into the small hours. We can spare an hour or so.'

'But won't Helena notice if you're not there?'

'It is to be hoped that Witherspoon will reassure her.' He sounded as though he was laughing. 'It is to be hoped that he has missed you, too, and is feeling anxious.'

'I don't suppose...' began Louisa doubtfully.

'My dear girl, of course he has missed you. How could he fail to do so? That is a charming dress you are wearing.'

Louisa drew a calming breath. If her companion was trying to needle her she would ignore him. Her 'Thank you' was straight from the freezer.

It was disconcerting when he said, 'I'm sorry, that was a nasty thing to say. Your dress is charming, but so are you, Louisa—by far the most beautiful woman there. It won't be just your Percy missing you; every man there will be wondering where you have got to.'

Louisa closed her mouth, which had fallen open in

amazement. 'Well, I never… It doesn't sound like you at all.'

'It must be the night air and all this extra activity. If Rosie is in bed, do you suppose you could make some sort of a meal? I'll make the toast.'

'Eggs,' said Louisa. 'Bacon, perhaps? There may be some soup we can warm up. Baked beans… Perhaps you don't eat those?'

'Why not? There's nothing quicker or more filling when I'm called out at night and I've missed dinner.'

Louisa sat silent. This was a side to Dr Gifford she hadn't discovered. He was quite human after all.

Shortly after he turned in at his own gate and stopped before his door. The house was in darkness save for a dim light in the hall. He unlocked the door and ushered her in, and at the same time Bellow came hurrying to meet them, and Rosie, wrapped in a cosy red dressing gown, started towards them.

'Sorry if we woke you, Rosie,' said the doctor. 'Someone was taken ill at the ball and we took her home. Go back to bed, my dear; we're going to have something to eat and then go back to the Woodleys'.'

Rosie smiled. 'There's plenty in the fridge, Mr Thomas.' She eyed Louisa. 'That's a pretty dress, Miss Howarth, fit for a pretty young lady, if I may say so.'

'Thank you, Rosie. You don't mind if I make sandwiches or something?'

'Lor' bless you, of course not.' She nodded at the pair of them. 'I'm off to bed, then. Mind you lock up when you go.'

The doctor said, 'Yes,' in a meek voice.

The kitchen was warm and welcoming, with the Aga damped down for the night, the great dresser against one wall and the solid table at its centre. There was a tabby cat asleep in a basket, and Bellow got back into his once he saw that there was no late-night walk intended. But, well concealed behind the cupboards and shelves and copper saucepans, Louisa discovered a massive fridge.

'Scrambled eggs and smoked salmon?' she asked. 'Brown bread and butter, toast—a Welsh rarebit? A pork pie. Does Rosie make them herself?'

'Yes. We can spare just under an hour, so start cooking, Louisa.'

'Yes, but which?'

He sounded surprised. 'Why, the lot, of course.'

Louisa was a good cook; the scrambled eggs were done to creamy perfection, the salmon just sufficient, brown bread and butter cut very thin, black pepper and lemon, and then the Welsh rarebit, bubbling crisply on the doctor's toast. They ate the pork pie, too, and washed the whole lot down with mugs of coffee.

They ate in a companionable silence broken only by a few desultory remarks about the evening's activities. They had both been there so there was no point in talking about it. They agreed that Rosie's pork pie was something not to be missed, and Louisa observed, 'You really have everything, Dr Gifford...'

He poured the last of the coffee. 'Not everything, Louisa. And isn't it about time to stop calling me Dr Gifford? My name is Thomas.'

'Well, since you've started calling me Louisa, I suppose I could call you Thomas. But not when we're at work.'

'A wise decision. Do you wish to go back to the Woodleys'? Or shall I take you back to your flat?'

'Oh, the Woodleys', I think, then I can explain to Percy.' She got up from the table and wrapped one of Rosie's pinnies around her. 'I'll wash—you wipe. You'll have to explain to Helena...'

She shouldn't have said that; he gave her a blank look and said silkily, 'Helena knows the Davidsons quite well. Naturally she will be concerned.'

A polite snub. He had invited her to call him Thomas, but that hadn't meant that they could say what they liked to each other. She said, coolly polite, 'How very fortunate it is that it is such a lovely night for the Woodleys' ball; rain would have cast rather a damper on it.'

He agreed gravely, a gleam of amusement in his eyes.

The kitchen restored to its pristine state, Louisa discarded her apron, knelt to give Bellow a hug and declared herself ready to go. She was on the floor, her arms around the dog, her skirts billowing round her, when Thomas, shrugging himself into his jacket, asked, 'You don't want to do your hair or your face or rearrange anything?'

She got to her feet. 'Oh, am I untidy? Is my nose shining? And my hair...'

He stood staring at her. 'As far as I can see, you look as though you have just come out of a bandbox. Let's go.'

He parked the car in front of the Woodleys' grand entrance and they went in together. 'I think if we were to dance and mingle with everyone else we should look less conspicuous.'

He didn't wait for her to agree but swung her onto the floor. They circled the room once and were halfway round it again before they saw Percy and Helena dancing. But before they could get near them Felicity, in the arms of a dour, red-faced man, was beside them.

'There you are. Where have you been? You missed supper.'

'One of the guests was taken ill—nothing serious, but she needed to go home,' said the doctor smoothly. 'Louisa kindly came with us and saw her safely into her bed.'

'Who was it?' Felicity looked at them in turn. 'Oh, I'm not to know, is that it? Oh, well, I'll find out for myself.'

She was danced away, and the doctor began to weave his way between the dancers to where Percy and Helena were standing, deep in talk.

Helena saw them first. 'Thomas, where have you been? And Louisa?' Her eyes narrowed. 'You missed supper...'

'Mary Davidson was taken ill; it was a question of getting her home to her own doctor as soon as possible. Louisa kindly came with us and saw her safely into bed and we waited until her own doctor came.'

'Why didn't you find me and tell me?'

'There wasn't time, and Mrs Woodley asked us to say nothing—it might have upset the guests.'

'What's wrong with her, anyway? Mary was always a silly girl—no stamina,' Helena said spitefully.

'She had plenty of stamina this evening,' said Louisa tartly. 'And we hope the baby is safe.' She added, 'I thought that you were a friend of Mary?'

Under her perfect make-up Helena went red. 'Oh, the poor dear, if only I had known. You should have fetched me, darling.' She turned her lovely blue eyes

to the doctor. 'After all, she needed a friend, not just
anyone…'

'How fortunate that it was Louisa and not just anyone,' said the doctor quietly.

'I must say,' said Percy, anxious to get a word in,
'I think it is most inconsiderate of you to go off like
that without a word to me, Louisa. I was beginning
to worry about you.'

'But you didn't notice that I wasn't here, did you,
Percy? So no harm's done. I'd like to dance.'

She smiled brilliantly at Helena and the doctor, and
floated away in Percy's arms. He talked gravely and
at some length as they danced, pointing out her shortcomings in a reasonable voice. 'You might take a les-
son from Helena,' he pointed out. 'There is nothing
boisterous about her; she is so self-possessed, and her
manners so quiet and pleasant.'

'You sound like something out of one of the
Brontës' books,' remarked Louisa. She laughed, and
then suddenly was angry. She stopped dancing so that
he came to a clumsy halt. 'How dare you, prosing on
and on like a puffed up Mr Barratt of Wimpole Street?
You had better go and find Miss Thornfold and explain how boisterous I am. Really, Percy, you had
better snap her up before Dr Gifford marries her.
You're so well suited.'

Percy looked surprised. 'Yes, I believe we are,' he
said complacently. 'As I was saying…'

'Not again. I'm going home, and if by any chance
you should feel that you should drive me back or get
me a taxi, don't bother. I've had several offers of a
lift home.' She uttered the fib with a casual certainty
which Percy, never the most perceptive of men, took
for the truth.

He said, 'Oh, well, if that's what you want. I must say this evening hasn't turned out as I had hoped...'

'No? I should have thought it was being much better than that.'

She turned on her heel and slipped away between the dancers, smiling and nodding to those she knew as she went. In the hall she saw Mrs Woodley.

'Louisa, thank you so much for your help. Thomas told me everything. I'm so grateful. Have you had supper? Where's Percy Witherspoon?'

'Mrs Woodley, I'm just going upstairs to tidy up a bit. I'm glad I could be of help. It's a lovely ball, and so successful.'

Mrs Woodley looked pleased. 'I'm glad it's going so well. I'm just going to make sure there is still plenty of food.'

Louisa nipped upstairs, found her wrap, peered over the banisters to make sure no one was about, and went back into the hall. She knew exactly what she was going to do—get hold of Hodge, the butler, and persuade him to find her a bike. The summer night wasn't dark, she wasn't nervous, and she knew the road. Half an hour's cycling, and she would be back at the flat.

It would be best, she thought, to go out of the front door and round to the side door leading to the kitchen; Hodge might be there. She found the door bolted. She should have thought of that, but there was still another way. She opened a door which would take her through the morning room and thence to the servants' quarters.

'I'll take you home,' said Dr Gifford quietly from somewhere behind her. 'I presume that's what your intention is?'

CHAPTER FIVE

Louisa knew now what it felt like to have her heart leap into her throat, a whimsical idea she had thought nonsense. She swallowed it back into its rightful place and said in an almost steady voice, 'Yes, but I have already made arrangements.'

'Rubbish, you've not had time. Is there a way out of this place if we go through here?'

She nodded. 'But I'm quite capable.'

'Yes, yes, you're very capable, but allow me to drive you back. Tell me, how did you intend to get home? A taxi?'

'No. I was going to borrow a bike from Hodge.'

The doctor, a man possessed of great self-control, just managed not to laugh. He didn't even smile. 'Ah, yes, of course.' Obedient to her pointing hand, he drew the bolts on a small door in the passage they had reached. It let them into a yard at the side of the house.

He closed the door behind them and waited while Louisa sensibly gathered her billowing skirts in a bunch. 'This way,' she told him, and plucked at his sleeve. 'Come along.'

The doctor, who hadn't enjoyed himself so much for a long time, came.

In the car Louisa said suddenly, 'I should have said something to Mrs Woodley.'

'I'll make your excuses for you when I get back.' He would have to think up a few of his own for

Helena, he reflected. He glanced sideways at Louisa, apparently so sensible and aloof in her manner, yet given to behaving quite out of character on the spur of the moment. And with a sharp tongue, too.

He told himself that it was a good thing he would only meet her at the consulting rooms; for some reason he found her disquieting.

His thoughts coloured his voice as he bade her goodbye at her flat, and Louisa was quick to hear it. The evening was something which was to be forgotten, a lapse in their detached manner towards each other. All the same, she asked, 'Do you want to come in and have a cup of coffee?'

His polite refusal chilled her.

She got ready for bed slowly, made herself a cup of cocoa and sat up in bed, drinking it. The evening hadn't been a total loss; Percy and Helena had met each other just as she had planned, and they had seemed attracted to each other, too. It was up to Thomas to prise his Helena loose from Percy if she became serious towards him, so Louisa had no regrets about her scheming. Helena wouldn't do for Thomas, anyone could see that—excepting him, of course.

'Men are silly!' said Louisa, and went to sleep.

She drove down to Stalbridge in the morning, for her planned visit to Aunt Martha. She lived alone, with two cats and an old dog, and liked a good gossip. Besides, Louisa didn't feel like seeing Felicity for a day or two; there would be too many questions asked. It was a lovely morning, and she wished that the drive was more than the thirty miles or so ahead of her. She knew that she would be welcome. All the same she stowed a bottle of wine in the back of the car and stopped in Shaftesbury to buy a box of chocolates—Aunt Martha's weakness.

Stalbridge, a large village tucked away from the main road, looked peaceful, drowsing in Sunday quiet, and Aunt Martha's house, in a quiet lane off its main street, looked just as peaceful. It was old, sturdily built and was surrounded by a garden crowded with flowers and shrubs. Aunt Martha was a keen gardener, and earned herself a small income from painting the flowers she grew. She had money of her own and lived comfortably, perfectly content with her life.

Louisa parked the car and went around the side of the house to the garden at the back. Her aunt was there, sitting under an apple tree, reading the Sunday papers. The cats and dog were with her, and they all got up as Louisa joined them.

'Louisa, how very nice to see you—you'll stay for lunch and tea, of course? It's quite some time since you were here. I hope you're going to tell me about the Woodleys' ball. You weren't sure if you were going when you phoned me.'

Louisa flopped down on the grass. 'Oh, this is lovely. Yes, I went to the ball.'

'Good. Run into the kitchen and fetch us some lemonade. And there are biscuits in a tin. Oh, and bring a chair as you come.' Aunt Martha added, 'It's cold lamb and salad for lunch and a rhubarb tart.'

The kitchen was small, very neat, clean and rather old-fashioned. Aunt Martha had no interest in modern gadgets. 'Give me a bowl and a wooden spoon,' she would tell anyone who remarked upon her lack of up-to-date equipment. Louisa poured the lemonade, found the biscuits, carried the tray into the garden, fetched a chair and sat down, feeling content.

Just looking at Aunt Martha was soothing; she was short and round, with rosy cheeks and twinkling brown eyes. Her hair was still a rich brown streaked with grey and she dressed it elegantly. She dressed well too—tweeds in the winter, cotton and linen in the summer. A 'little woman' made her clothes and, for as long as Louisa could remember, they had never varied in style.

Aunt Martha accepted a glass of lemonade and said abruptly, 'It's time you married. And not that Witherspoon man who's been dangling after you for years. Does he still?'

'Dangle? Well, until yesterday…' Louisa, her mouth full of biscuit, told Aunt Martha all about the ball and her schemes.

She mentioned the doctor as little as possible, which didn't prevent Aunt Martha from observing, 'He sounds quite a man, this doctor. Do you like him?'

'He doesn't like me,' said Louisa. 'He's going to marry Helena Thornfold; do you know her?'

'Thornfold,' mused her aunt. 'Knew her parents; never got on with them. If she's anything like her mother, he's in for a terrible time. A mean and spiteful woman—very pretty, though.'

'Helena is quite beautiful…'

'But mean and spiteful?' asked Aunt Martha shrewdly.

'Yes, she contrives to make me feel fat whenever we see each other.'

'Sour grapes, my dear. There's no fat on you, only curves where they ought to be.' Aunt Martha heaved herself out of her chair. 'Come and lay the table for me while I make a salad.'

Escorted by the cats and the dog, they went indoors and presently lunched in a leisurely fashion. Afterwards Louisa washed up before they went back to the garden, where she lay in the grass under the apple tree and dozed, to wake refreshed at the sound of her aunt's voice observing that there was a freshly baked lardy cake if she felt like tea.

She went back to Salisbury in the early evening, full of sun and fresh air, half-convinced that any life other than the simple one her aunt lived was not life at all.

She had supper and went to bed. At least Dr Gifford wouldn't be at Sir James's rooms until Wednesday; the less she saw of him, the better, although she wasn't sure why.

The first person she saw when she got to work in the morning was him.

His good morning was uttered in a preoccupied manner. 'Sir James is unable to get here until this afternoon; he has asked me to take over for the morning. Will you let me have the patients' notes as quickly as possible?'

He was on the phone when she took them in and laid them on the desk, but before she reached the door he had put it down.

'Is there anything I should know about this morning's patients?'

'Peggy Matthews, she's ten and very bright; likes to know what's happening.' Louisa paused for thought. 'Her mother's a timid lady, expects the worst. There's a tin of toffees in the left-hand drawer of the desk; Sir James gives Peggy one before she goes.'

Dr Gifford sat back in his chair. 'What a mine of useful information you are,' he observed. 'Thank you, Louisa.'

'Not at all, sir,' snapped Louisa. She resisted a desire to slam the door hard as she went out.

And after that she was too busy to think about anything else but dealing with the post, the appointment book and the telephone, until Sir James came bustling in as she was putting on the kettle for her lunch. Mrs Grant had gone shopping, and Jilly spent her lunch hour in a coffee shop in one of the small side streets. Louisa intended to eat her sandwiches quickly and go for a brisk walk. It was amazing what a lot one could do in an hour if one planned it carefully.

Sir James put an end to all that. He greeted her breezily, told her to turn off the kettle and come into his consulting room. 'Ten minutes' work, Miss Howarth. I'll dictate while I have a few moments to spare.'

Dr Gifford was still there, standing by the window, whistling, his hands in his pockets.

'Ah, Thomas—good of you to take over. I have had a most interesting morning with Professor Lutvik; you remember him? We intend to get together again. In the meanwhile, he suggests a seminar. A good idea, don't you think? Miss Howarth, sit down. You have your notebook? Good. I must get his plans for it down while they are still fresh in my memory.'

He sat down at his desk and Louisa waited, pencil poised. But Sir James had started to talk to his colleague, and she sat, outwardly calm, inwardly impatient, her stomach rumbling. She would have to gobble her sandwiches and forego her walk. Ten minutes went by while the two men talked, and since their conversation was carried out mainly in medical terms she gave up listening. But presently there was a brief lull in their talk.

'This is my lunch hour,' said Louisa.

They both looked at her, Sir James in surprise, Dr Gifford with no expression whatsoever, but he was laughing at her behind it; she was sure of that.

'My dear Miss Howarth. Of course—how forgetful of me.' Sir James looked at Thomas. 'We'll talk about this later—must you go back at once?'

'I'm not needed until the five o'clock surgery at Cranborne. There is plenty of time before the afternoon patients come.'

'Yes, yes, of course. Splendid. Now, Miss Howarth…'

With constant interruptions while he changed his mind, it took fifteen more minutes to dictate. Finally he said, 'If you'll get that typed up for me? I don't suppose you're very busy this afternoon.' He smiled kindly at her. 'Now, off you go and have your lunch…'

There was exactly ten minutes left of her lunch hour. Mrs Grant, bustling in with her shopping, said, 'You're back early…'

Louisa gave a snort. 'I haven't been,' she said, and went to put the kettle on.

Sir James settled himself at his desk. 'Miss Howarth doesn't seem quite herself,' he remarked.

'Possibly she is hungry, and she has barely ten minutes of her lunch hour left.'

'My dear fellow, how thoughtless of me. She had better have the hour now; I'm sure Mrs Grant and Jilly can manage. You've had lunch?'

'No, no, not yet. Supposing I take Miss Howarth with me? There's a small café close by, isn't there?'

'A splendid idea, Thomas. That will allow her to get back into her usual calm frame of mind.' He added, 'I shall want her to stay late this afternoon.'

'Then the sooner we go, the better.'

Louisa wasn't quite sure how he did it, but under Mrs Grant's and Jilly's interested eyes he prised her from the almost boiling kettle and marched her gently but firmly into the street.

'There's a small place close by,' he observed cheerfully. 'We might get egg and chips or something similar. I don't know about you, but I had breakfast hours ago. And don't fuss about time; Sir James said that you were to have your lunch hour.'

'Yes, but this is quite unnecessary, Dr Gifford.'

He said, with perfect gravity, 'Your blood sugar mustn't be allowed to get too low and you doubtless have a busy afternoon ahead of you. Ah, here we are.'

It was a very small café, catering for those who needed food that could be eaten quickly. The furnishings were basic, but the paper tablecloths were clean and so was the weedy youth behind the small counter. They sat at a table in the window and the youth came at once.

'The sausage and mash is all gone—you're a bit late. I could do you a couple of eggs on toast with baked beans and a nice pot of tea?'

Dr Gifford glanced at Louisa. 'Does that sound all right to you, Louisa?' And when she nodded the youth sped away to return in a few minutes with a large brown pot of tea, cups and saucers, milk and sugar.

'Five minutes for the food,' he told them. 'Plenty more hot water if you want it.'

The tea was strong, and Louisa drank it thankfully. The doctor drank his, too, remarking casually, 'Such a reviving drink, isn't it? Strong enough to bring anyone back from death's door.' And in the same breath he asked, 'Do you like your work, Louisa?'

'Yes, yes, of course I do. Sir James is nice to work for, and I like Mrs Grant and Jilly.' She tried to think of something else to say and couldn't, so it was as well that the youth brought the eggs and beans—generous portions, nicely cooked and piping hot.

The doctor, passing the pepper and salt, tried to imagine Helena in Louisa's place and couldn't. Somehow baked beans and Helena didn't go together, whereas he had to admit that Louisa looked exactly right, polishing off her piled-up plate with unselfconscious appetite.

Presently she sat back, her plate empty. 'I was hungry,' she said simply.

'And there is quite a lot of you to keep nourished,' observed the doctor. 'Would you like another pot of tea or one of those buns under that glass dome on the counter?'

He was secretly amused that she had taken his remarks in good part. Indeed, now that she was no longer hungry, she had forgotten to be haughty.

'No, thank you. I enjoyed that. I must go back. It was kind of you to bring me here.'

She half expected him to say that it had been a pleasure or something similar, but he said nothing at all, only lifted an eyebrow at the youth, who came with the bill.

'Food OK?' he wanted to know.

'It was delicious,' said Louisa, 'and very well cooked. Did you cook it?'

'No, me ma does the cooking.' He accepted the doctor's tip with a gratified smirk. 'Come again any time.'

Which wasn't very likely, thought Louisa, at least not with the doctor.

It took them only a few minutes to go back to the consulting rooms. It wasn't until they were going up the stairs that Dr Gifford remarked casually, 'Witherspoon wasn't too upset by your absence on Saturday evening?'

She turned to look at him. 'I don't know. I haven't seen him since.'

And at his small faintly mocking smile, she added coldly, 'Was Helena very put out?'

He disconcerted her by saying seriously, 'Oh, yes, very. How fortunate that your Percy was there to take my place.'

'He is *not* my Percy,' said Louisa.

Dr Gifford went away during the afternoon, and Louisa, watching him go, wondered when he would come again. He had made no mention of it and Sir James had gone off to the hospital at the end of the afternoon, observing briskly that they appeared to have a busy week ahead of them.

She went to see Felicity after she had had an evening meal, and found her alone. Her stepmother, bored with her own company, was pleased to see her.

'I'm exhausted,' she explained. 'We didn't get back from the Woodleys' until almost three o'clock and yesterday I went out to lunch, and Percy came round in the evening. I'm dining at the Thornfolds' tomorrow and I do want to look my best. Are you going?'

'Me? No. I hardly know Helena or her parents.'

'But you do know Thomas Gifford,' said Felicity slyly.

'No, I don't. We see each other at Sir James's and I've done some work for him.'

'But on Saturday night you were hours away from the ball...'

'It was hardly a social occasion.'

Felicity frowned. 'Such a tiresome thing to happen—the silly girl should have stayed at home.'

Louisa didn't answer. Mary Davidson might be young, and she had been frightened, but she hadn't been silly. Louisa said instead, 'What will you wear?'

A safe topic, discussed endlessly.

'Will you drive yourself there?'

'Percy is taking me. He had a last-minute invitation from Helena. She's quite taken with him.' Felicity giggled. 'I wonder what Thomas Gifford thinks of that. Of course, it's his fault; he shouldn't go off like that and leave her. They were actually dancing together.'

'He's a doctor,' said Louisa. 'She will have to get used to him going off at a moment's notice when an emergency crops up.'

Felicity laughed. 'He's got a partner. When they marry there's no reason why he shouldn't take another partner and have more leisure. Helena likes a social life.'

A badly matched pair, reflected Louisa; how on earth did they hope to be happily married? Of course, if they were in love...but they weren't. She had no reason to think that, but she felt it to be true. If only Percy...

'You look as though you're plotting something,' said Felicity.

'No, no. I just remembered all the extra work Sir
James wants me to do this week. There's to be a seminar...'

'Oh, darling, don't bore me with details.'

'Well, I won't, and anyway I must go back to the
flat. I'll go and see Biddy as I leave.'

She bent to kiss her stepmother's cheek. 'Have you
paid her?'

'Oh, dear. I can't remember. Be a darling and see
to it for me, will you?'

'I saw to it last time; you still owe me. I'll pay her
now if you give me the money.'

Felicity reached for her handbag—crocodile
leather; it must have cost at least six months of
Biddy's wages. 'You know, Louisa, sometimes I think
you're getting a bit hard. You won't get a husband
unless you change—it's a good thing you've got this
job and money coming to you. At least you'll be independent.'

Louisa said cheerfully, 'Well, you won't need to
worry about me, will you?'

Biddy was in the kitchen, labelling the pots of jam
she had been making.

They had a cup of tea while Louisa listened to
Biddy's gossip and admired the new hat she had
bought herself.

'When I go to the pub I like a good hat,' said
Biddy. 'There's a couple of pots of jam for you, Miss
Louisa. I hope you're eating proper.'

Louisa assured her that she was, gave the nice old
thing a hug and went back to her flat. There was still
an hour or so before she could go to bed; she sat by
the window and applied her wits to the problem of Dr
Gifford. It was obvious to her now that he mustn't

marry Helena. Percy was the answer, of course, but that meant that he and Helena must meet as often as possible.

How to contrive that?

Of course, if Thomas were to go away for a time… But that wasn't likely. Meeting socially was the answer, as often as possible, and perhaps there was the possibility of Thomas being called away to a private patient. After all, Sir James had been away for several days, so why shouldn't Thomas go? She must stop calling him Thomas…

She went to bed presently, her mind made up to do something about it, although she didn't go too deeply into her reasons for doing so.

She wasn't deterred by his absence for the rest of the week, but she was disappointed. Seeing that she had his future welfare at heart, she wanted to keep tabs on him. It was Sir James, affable after an easy morning, who told her that he was going to the theatre that evening to see the local dramatic society's play.

'My wife enjoys that sort of thing,' Sir James told her. 'There will be quite a party of us—the Woodleys and the Thornfolds and, of course Dr Gifford and Helena Thornfold. I'm surprised your stepmother didn't mention it; she will be there—and young Witherspoon, of course.'

'You'll enjoy it, sir,' said Louisa cheerfully. 'Do you know anyone acting in it?'

'As a matter of fact, our youngest daughter—just a small part.'

As she was leaving, he asked, 'Surely it is time for you to have a holiday, Miss Howarth? Have you any plans?'

'Vague ones, sir. I've an aunt and uncle living in Scotland; they've asked me to visit them.'

'Well, decide when you want to go and let me know. Will two weeks be enough?'

'Yes, thank you. I'll give them a ring and make a date.'

It would be delightful to go to Scotland, but anything could happen in the two weeks she'd be away. Helena might marry Dr Gifford—something which Louisa found most unsatisfactory. She would have to think of something, some way in which Percy could see more of Helena.

She worried away at it like a dog with a bone, and finally went to bed that night with no idea as to how that might be done.

It was three o'clock in the morning when she woke and sat up in bed. A picnic! Felicity and Percy, of course, any of the Woodleys who felt like coming, the Davidsons if they were up to it, and Helena and Thomas.

'Ideal,' said Louisa, and went back to sleep.

In the morning she phoned her aunt in Scotland and arranged to visit them in two weeks' time, settled dates with Sir James, and that evening went to see Felicity to tell her the plans for a picnic.

'Where?'

'There's that nice wooded bit around Woodminton, and there's the river. The cars can be left in the lane, and it's only a few yards to the meadows. Just right for a picnic.'

'Don't expect me to organise anything. Will you see to the food? And for heaven's sake have enough to drink. Who are you asking?' And after a thoughtful pause, 'Why are you doing it, Louisa?'

Louisa turned a guileless face to her. 'Well, it's such lovely weather. Once it breaks we'll all regret not having enjoyed it more. People like picnics as long as they don't have to arrange them.'

'Well, it's quite a good idea. Who will you ask?'

Louisa told her.

'When is it to be?'

'Well, not this weekend but the next one. I'll phone everyone this evening or tomorrow.'

Everyone accepted. Louisa left Helena until last and made no mention of the doctor.

'I shall bring Thomas with me, of course,' said Helena. 'I suppose you don't mind if he comes?'

'Of course not.' Louisa was careful to be casual. 'I wasn't sure if he would be free.'

'I'll make sure that he is. He'll have to fetch me and bring me home.'

Before Helena put the phone down she asked if Percy would be there. Louisa was pleased about that. At least she would be able to see if the rapport between Helena and Percy had deepened before she went to Scotland. She sat down and made a list of everything necessary to make the picnic a success.

The doctor came to the consulting rooms twice during the following week but, beyond exchanging polite good mornings and good afternoons, they had nothing to say to each other.

I don't know why I bother, thought Louisa. He doesn't like me and he won't thank me for saving him from that woman. He might not want to be saved, of course. It was a pity she didn't know him well enough to ask him...

Saturday dawned sunny and warm. Just right, thought Louisa, packing hampers and loading bottles into cool-boxes. She had spent a busy week but it would be worthwhile. She loaded her car, piled in rugs and cushions and a couple of folding chairs she had borrowed from Felicity, and set off.

The picnic site wasn't far, and was reached through narrow country lanes, but she had chosen the spot well. There was plenty of room for the cars to park on the wide grass verge, and there was a gate into the field. Some of the trees bordering it had been cut down from time to time, so the stumps would make ideal seats, softened by the cushions.

She unpacked the car and arranged everything to her liking, before wandering down to the stream. It was narrow and not deep and there were stepping stones to the other side, and beyond that, some way off, the high stone wall bounding one of the estates around Salisbury.

It was very quiet; somewhere in the distance she could hear a tractor, and sheep and lambs bleating, but presently she heard a car's engine so she went back to the gate to welcome the first of her guests. The Woodleys. Everyone else came then—the Davidsons, Felicity and Percy and, last of all, Helena and Dr Gifford. Helena was too elaborately dressed and she looked cross. The doctor, dressed in elderly trousers and an open-necked shirt and still looking elegant, greeted her with a friendly nod. 'A lovely spot, isn't it? Do you come here often?'

'Occasionally; I like the stream.'

'I hope there aren't any ants,' said Helena. She gave a little trill of laughter. 'If I were to get bitten... I have such a delicate skin.'

She looked at Louisa's unmade-up face with its freckles across her pretty nose. 'I'm not like you—a great healthy woman.'

Louisa said gently, 'It must be a trial to you if you are not healthy. My granny used to say, "Remember, Louisa, health not wealth". Come over here and sit on one of these tree stumps—here's an extra cushion—and you can lean against this tree; it's nicely shaded. I'm going to pour the drinks—what would you like? There's white wine, tonic water, orange juice and beer.'

As she talked, Louisa installed Helena on her cushions with all the solicitude of a nurse looking after an invalid, taking no notice of Dr Gifford at all. He stayed with Helena for a few minutes and then wandered off to say hello to everyone, and then helped carry round the drinks while Louisa unpacked the food.

It had been worth the effort, she thought an hour later. The tiny sausage rolls, the vol-au-vents with smoked salmon, the onion tarts and the miniature spring rolls had all been eaten. So had the French bread, the butter and the Brie, and there wasn't a morsel of ice cream left.

The good food and drinks had loosened everyone's tongues; there was a gratifying babble of voices and a good deal of laughter and, best of all, Percy was sitting beside Helena, their heads together, deep in talk. And Thomas? He was lying on the grass beside Mary Davidson's chair, and Ricky was with Felicity.

With the help of the Woodleys she packed up the remains of the picnic and, when urged to do so, went across the field to the stream. It looked inviting on the other side; worth a look, said the youngest of the

Woodleys, so that Louisa promptly sat down, took off her sandals and followed them over the stepping stones. She bunched her long skirt up around her knees, and paused halfway across to dabble her feet in the water.

Dr Gifford, watching her as he listened to Mary's mild chatter, thought that he had never seen anyone as beautiful. The wholly unexpected thought that he wanted her for his wife took him by surprise, and was instantly suppressed as ridiculous. She was a tiresome girl, always speaking her mind instead of holding her tongue, sitting at her desk looking through him with her enormous grey eyes.

Mary's voice recalled him to reality. 'She's such a dear, and she never pretends, if you know what I mean. I'm glad she's got that flat; it must have been pretty dull for her, living with Mrs Howarth. I mean, her stepmother is such a glamorous person, isn't she? With hosts of friends. Oh, I know Louisa went out a lot, but they weren't her friends, if you see what I mean.'

'I didn't know that you knew her.'

'Well, no, I didn't, but people talk, you know? Everyone likes her, and she's so clever. All this food—she made everything herself...'

'Indeed?' said Thomas, and brushed aside an unbidden picture of Louisa in his kitchen. He couldn't substitute it with one of Helena, for she had never been into his kitchen. Kitchens were for housekeepers and cooks.

'Of course, when we are married,' Helena had told him, 'I'll go every day and tell Rosie what has to be done and decide on meals.' She had leaned up and kissed his cheek. 'I'm a drawing room girl, darling.'

Lying there beside Mary, watching Louisa strolling on the other side of the stream with the three Woodleys, Thomas wondered when he had first become aware that he was disillusioned. He clamped down on that thought, too.

The picnic broke up before tea time. Tea from a flask never tasted the same as tea from a pot, and Louisa had decided that she didn't want to spoil the success of the picnic. Everyone went, declaring that they had had a lovely time, and Helena and Dr Gifford were the last to go.

Helena kept him waiting while she rubbed cream into her arms, which she declared had been burned by the sun. She said with a spiteful titter, 'I know it seems fussy to you, Louisa, but I go out such a lot, and I like to take care of my appearance.'

'I'm sure you do,' said Louisa, the polite hostess. 'Are you going out this evening?'

Helena cast a vexed look at the doctor. 'Thomas was supposed to be taking me out to dine and dance, but, of course, he has to go to that wretched hospital. Luckily, Percy is free and offered to take me. Such a thoughtful man. I'm surprised that you don't appreciate him.'

Louisa said in a cool voice, 'Even if you are surprised, I don't think it is any business of yours, Helena. Are you ready? I should think Dr Gifford is getting impatient.'

He wasn't only impatient, he was angry, too. In the car he said in a deceptively mild voice, 'You were rude to Louisa, and spiteful.'

Helena rounded on him. 'I'll say what I like,

Thomas—I had no idea she was such a friend of yours.'

'Louisa is a trusted and hard-working member of Sir James's staff. She is not a friend, but you have no right to belittle her.'

'You were listening…'

'Your voice when you are annoyed is shrill, Helena.'

They drove the rest of the way in silence, and at her parents' house she got out of the car without a backward glance, brushing past him without a word, too. Only at the door she turned to shout at him.

'I hope you have a very busy evening and that everything goes wrong for you and your beastly patients.'

A pity Louisa couldn't have been there to hear that. Back in her flat, clearing away the debris from the picnic, she thought that it had been a success, and certainly Percy and Helena were fulfilling her hopes. It was a pity that Thomas appeared quite unmoved by their friendship; he must feel very sure of Helena, despite her tantrums.

Well, she had done her best. In a week's time she would be in Scotland with no way of finding out how things were progressing. She had lost, she thought. Surely a man seeing his fiancée becoming more and more friendly with another man would have done something about it, and either they would have parted or made it up. He must have seen for himself…

She made a pot of tea, had a shower, put on an old cotton dress and tied herself into a pinny. She would cook something for her supper and then look through

her wardrobe and decide what she would take to
Scotland.

She was scrubbing new potatoes when the doorbell
rang and, when she opened it, there was Dr Gifford,
taking up every inch of the tiny hall, and tucked carefully in his arm was a very small and dirty kitten.

CHAPTER SIX

LOUISA looked at the small, pathetic furry face and then at Dr Gifford. 'The kitchen. I'll get a towel...'

He laid the scrap on it. 'I'll take a look before we clean him up. He was on the side of the road. Do you have something soft? And warm water. And warm milk... He's skin and bone.'

The kitten didn't make a sound as he was examined with gentle hands.

'Nothing broken as far as I can tell. Let's try him with some milk.'

It was scoffed with speed, and the doctor began to clean the little beast's fur. It was matted and muddy, and he worked slowly, pausing while the kitten had a second saucer of milk. Presently, the worst of the mud and dirt gently wiped away, it went to sleep.

'A box,' said Louisa. 'I have the very thing.' She provided a hat box, an elaborate thing of coloured stripes but roomy and deep enough to keep the kitten safe. She lined it with newspaper and an old woolly scarf and took it into the kitchen.

Only then did she ask, 'Where did you find him? And I thought you were going to the hospital.' She glanced at Thomas's calm face. 'If you're on your way to join Helena, I'll look after the kitten.'

'I was on my way to see you.'

'Me? Why?'

'I can hardly take over from Witherspoon in the middle of dinner, can I?' He lifted an eyebrow at her. 'I told Rosie that I wouldn't be back until late, but I

was quickly finished at the hospital. I thought we
might go out to dinner?'

'You and me? Whatever for? Besides, I'm not going to leave him.'

She put a gentle hand on the little creature's head.

'You don't mince your words, do you, Louisa? If
I may borrow your hat box, we will be on our way.'

'I didn't mean that. My wretched tongue. Only you
surprised me—I mean, asking me to have dinner with
you. I'm sorry; don't go. If you'd like to stay, I'll
cook supper.' She added, 'If you stay, you could make
sure that the kitten will be all right.'

'Thank you. I'm not spoiling your evening?'

'No, no, of course not. There's a bottle of white
wine in the cupboard by the fireplace; will you open
it? Will you eat lamb chops?'

'With a good appetite. Where do you keep the cork-
screw?'

Louisa, busy in the kitchen, called through the open
door. 'Will you shell the peas for me? And is the
kitten all right?'

She came into the sitting room with a colander in
her hand. 'Here you are. Give yourself a glass of
wine, won't you? And pour me a glass; I'll be back
presently.'

Thomas shucked the peas and enjoyed himself. It
occurred to him that she had shown no surprise when
he had knocked on her door but had admitted him as
though he were an old friend, which, considering their
wariness with each other, was strange... He finished
the peas and took them into the kitchen, then asked
meekly what he should do next.

Louisa had put the potatoes on to cook and heated
the grill ready for the chops. There was some pastry
over from the vol-au-vents she had made for the pic-

nic, and she rolled it out, lined a flan case, sliced apples into it and popped it into the oven. There was cream in the fridge, and she would make coffee later. She took the peas from him.

'You could lay the table, please. Knives and forks and a tablecloth in the top drawer of the dresser. Is the kitten all right?'

'Sleeping. Shall I bring your wine here?'

'Please. Bring yours, too.'

It occurred to her then that it seemed the most natural thing in the world for her to be cooking their supper while the doctor, very much at home, sat on the kitchen table, one comforting hand on the kitten, while they debated the many methods of cooking the potato. And presently they ate their meal, talking about this and that. She was careful not to mention Helena, anxious not to spoil the evening. As for Thomas, he had nothing to say about himself but discussed mundane events in a casual manner which disarmed her entirely.

'What shall we do with this little chap?' he asked her as they watched the kitten polishing off another saucer of milk.

'I'll have him,' said Louisa, and added, 'But not for a week or two. I'm going on holiday.'

'Somewhere where you can't take him?' asked Thomas carelessly.

'Scotland. The Highlands. All that distance—and he might get lost.'

'Then supposing I have him until you return? Bellow will be delighted, and so will Rosie. When do you go?'

'Next Saturday. I meant to drive up but that would waste two days so I'll go by train.'

'It should be delightful at this time of year—a few
weeks in the Highlands.'

'Only two. I've an aunt and uncle living near
Torridon. It's a small village—Shieldaig—by the
loch. It's very quiet and the country around is beautiful.'

Thomas, careful not to show interest, drew her attention to the kitten, who, sensing that life was worth
living after all, was making feeble efforts to wash
himself.

They washed the supper dishes together and presently the doctor went away, the hat box carefully held
under one arm. At the door he thanked Louisa for his
supper. 'A very pleasant evening,' he observed.

'Yes, it was,' Louisa agreed. 'And I suppose next
time I see you you'll look at me as though I wasn't
there!'

'Oh, dear—do I do that?' He bent and kissed her
cheek, and had gone down the stairs and out of the
house before she could draw breath.

'Well, I never did!' said Louisa, and put up a hand
to touch her cheek. 'He must have forgotten who I
was for a moment.'

All the same, it had been a nice ending to her day.

In the morning, after matins in the cathedral, she
walked back with Felicity.

'That was quite a pleasant picnic yesterday, Louisa;
everyone enjoyed themselves.' She gave a little laugh.
'Percy was delighted to see more of Helena
Thornfold. I must say, they get on frightfully well. I
suppose Thomas doesn't mind—well, he must expect
it, mustn't he? She's so lovely. What are you doing
for the rest of the day? I'm out to lunch.'

'I'll start getting ready for my holiday. There won't

be much time during the week, and I want to get away on Saturday early; it's a long journey.'

'You'll be bored stiff,' said Felicity. 'I went there once with your father. All that stillness, and the mountains...' She gave a delicate shudder. 'So frightening.'

They parted then.

'Enjoy your day, darling,' Felicity smiled. 'Perhaps you'll meet a nice man in that God-forsaken place.'

Dr Gifford came on Tuesday afternoon, just in time for the first of the patients. Sir James had gone to the hospital and wouldn't be back until the following morning, leaving a message asking Dr Gifford to phone him after four o'clock. The message had been left with Louisa, who was slightly uneasy at the idea of meeting the doctor again. Which was silly, she told herself, so that when he arrived she wished him a composed good afternoon and was disconcerted when he stopped by her desk.

'Good afternoon, Louisa.' He stared at her so hard that she went pink and frowned. He smiled then, and said loudly enough for Mrs Grant and Jilly to hear, 'You see, I am endeavouring to mend my manners. And the kitten is doing well.'

'Oh, good—that's nice,' said Louisa, for once at a loss for words, before becoming the perfect receptionist again. 'Sir James asked me to ask you to phone him after four o'clock at the hospital.'

He nodded and went into his consulting room, and Jilly hardly waited for the door to close before asking what all that had been about.

'What's wrong with his manners? They're lovely— he held the door open for me the other day... And what was that about a kitten?'

Mrs Grant said sharply, 'Jilly, don't be nosy. Here's

the first patient. Make sure the examination room is ready.'

The afternoon was busy, but the last patient went before five o'clock and very shortly after Dr Gifford went away, wishing them good day as he went. This time he didn't look at Louisa but walked straight past her desk.

Back to square one, reflected Louisa, her feelings hurt.

They would have had a tremendous uplift if she could have joined the two doctors sitting in the austere room set aside for the use of the medical staff at the hospital. Sir James was talking.

'The seminar is next week—Wednesday—at Glasgow Infirmary, then if you would go and see Professor Lutvik in Edinburgh? I'll give you his address. And while you're there you could go to Inverness. I've already written to explain that I must stay here until my wife is better. I had a very civil phone message—he is perfectly willing to see you in my stead.

'His convalescence has gone smoothly and he will be going back to his own country very shortly. I was against him coming here when I was treating him, but it has been a good idea. As far as his own countrymen know, he's still recovering at his home there; he'll go back fit and well and very few people will be any the wiser. How long can you spare?'

'I've a locum to help out. Ten days or a fortnight.'

'You'll be in Scotland at the same time as Miss Howarth.'

'So I shall,' said Thomas blandly.

Sir James had warned him that he might have to go to Scotland in his place some days ago, and he had expected to spend no more than four days there, but now he intended to stay. Inverness wasn't too long a drive from Shieldaig and he wanted to see Louisa, spend days with her.

Perhaps if he did that he would be able to convince himself that his growing interest in her was no more than a passing fantasy, encouraged by Helena's increasing demands that he should give up a large part of his practice and concentrate on private patients, so that he could play a larger part in her social life. It was only in the last few months that she had allowed him to see the kind of life that she intended they should lead, and when he had flatly refused she had sulked for days...

Driving himself home presently, he was forced to admit that he no longer loved Helena. Perhaps he never had; they had known each other for some time and she had made no secret of wanting to marry him. She was charming and beautiful and they shared friends and a similar lifestyle; it had seemed the logical thing to do, to become engaged and settle down, have a wife and children.

Only Helena had made it clear that, although she was prepared to have one child, she had no intention of having more. Thomas hadn't said much at the time, confident that she would alter her ideas when they were married, but he'd soon realised that she meant what she'd said, just as she had refused to discuss their wedding. She was enjoying her carefree, idle life and she would marry him when she was ready. After all, she was very sure of him. Even if he had become a little disenchanted, he was an honourable man; he had promised to marry her.

Letting himself into his quiet house, he was greeted

by Bellow, and then set about the business of making the kitten comfortable.

Thomas thrust a problematical future to the back of his mind, took Bellow for a brisk walk and took himself off to bed. Never mind his own problems; tomorrow morning there would be his patients' problems to solve, and he must discuss several cases with his partner and talk to the locum. All the same, his last thoughts before he went to sleep were of Louisa.

Sir James told Louisa the following day that his wife was suffering from a severe attack of shingles, although he said nothing about Thomas going to Scotland. 'Do what you can to book patients for the mornings, Miss Howarth; I'd like to be as free as possible in the afternoons. Mrs Twist will be filling in for you as usual when you're away, so make sure she understands that, won't you?'

Louisa said that she would and pointed out that she had asked Mrs Twist to come on Friday afternoon for a quick résumé of what she might expect during the next two weeks.

'Good, good,' said Sir James. 'I hope you have an enjoyable holiday, Miss Howarth.'

'And I—all of us—hope that your wife is quickly well again, sir.'

Thomas came too, that day. There were more patients than usual, and beyond a quick greeting as he went through the waiting room he had nothing to say. Certainly he didn't look at Louisa, and he was still there when she, Mrs Grant and Jilly went home.

Only the next morning there was a note on her desk.

The kitten is thriving; Bellow is proving an excellent parent.

He could have told her that, it would have taken only a couple of seconds. The memory of the pleasant warmth of their evening together iced over; she had been a convenient port of call with the kitten and he had made use of it.

'Well, I don't care,' said Louisa. There wasn't anyone else there yet, so she said it again, loudly.

Two more days to go before her holiday. She filled her spare time in packing, booking her ticket, phoning her uncle and going to see Felicity and Biddy.

Felicity thought she was being very silly, going all that way to stay in a dull little village. 'You'll be bored,' she warned Louisa. 'And supposing it rains?'

'I shall go walking, and Torridon is less than eight miles away.'

'And what could you do there? Mark my words, you're going to be so pleased to be back here. Have you seen anything of Percy?'

'No. Should I have?'

'You only have yourself to blame; you've lost your chance there.' Her stepmother added, 'I met Helena this morning—we were both buying shoes. She's going to the races on Sunday. She hasn't told Thomas; she intends to surprise him, just ask him to take her for a drive and then drive to the race course. She's meeting friends there. He doesn't care for racing, but she's fed up with never going anywhere.'

'But she does go everywhere.'

'Yes, I know, what she meant was that she wants him to dangle beside her wherever she goes. She's so used to men falling for her and treating her like a film star that she resents him treating her like a human being.'

Louisa could think of several answers to that, none of them suitable, so she held her tongue.

Biddy was pleased to see her. 'Just this minute made a pot of tea,' she declared. 'Sit down, Miss Louisa, and tell me all the news.'

So Louisa sat for half an hour, describing the picnic in great detail.

'I'd as soon eat me dinner off a table,' said Biddy, 'with half a pint of bitter to wash it down. The missus said you're going to Scotland. Now, mind you enjoy yourself—happen there'll be some young folk there?'

'I'll send you a postcard,' Louisa promised.

There was no sign of Thomas during those two days, and, beyond telling her that his wife was getting a little better, Sir James had nothing to say to her.

She got the early-morning train on Saturday, very nicely dressed in an entirely suitable outfit—a fine jersey skirt and top and a little jacket in oatmeal— which would stand up to the long day ahead without creasing, and adapt itself to any change in the weather. And with a manageable suitcase and a shoulder bag which held everything she would possibly need for the journey.

And it was a long journey, although she had a comfortable window seat on the Intercity Express. By the time she changed trains at Glasgow and was on her way again she was getting tired. But the magnificent scenery made her forget that. The train skirted the last stretch of Loch Lomond and after that the country became increasingly enthralling—mountains in the distance, waterfalls, deep glens and scarcely a village to be seen. There were mountains all around now, and vast stretches of moorland until the train ran alongside Loch Treig and stopped briefly at Tullach Station.

Now Spean Bridge was only thirty miles away and

her long journey was almost over. Her uncle would be waiting for her there and they would drive the last eighty-odd miles to Shieldaig. Louisa tidied her hair and powdered her nose, glad that the journey was almost over, looking forward to two weeks of peace and pleasure with two people for whom she had a deep affection.

She allowed herself a moment in which to wonder what Thomas was doing, and then dismissed him from her mind. Despite her efforts he would marry Helena, because Helena had made up her mind to that, even if she did find Percy attractive. Well, Louisa had done her best and she hadn't succeeded. She should never have meddled in the first place. Thomas Gifford was old enough and wise enough to sort out his own life.

There was no time for more troubled thoughts; the train had pulled into the station, and there was Uncle Bob, looking like Father Christmas in tweeds, his voice booming a welcome, holding her in a vast embrace and then urging her out to the Land Rover.

'We'll have something to eat here in the town,' he told her. 'But no hanging about, mind, for your aunt will be waiting with a meal.'

He plied her with questions while they had tea and toast and thick slices of buttered bannock, and then they were on the road again, a main road which ran for some miles beside Loch Lochy before Bob turned onto the A87, going west. There were no villages now, an occasional inn, the glimpse of a loch, great sweeps of moorland, and everywhere mountains, and then, after thirty miles or so, Loch Duich and then Loch Carron.

'Almost home,' said Uncle Bob. 'Nothing much has changed since you were last here—three years? Time goes so quickly nowadays.'

'Two years, and it's all as beautiful as ever.' Louisa
stared around her. Not a house in sight. There were
forests, and any minute now they would see Loch
Shieldaig and the village. They had exchanged news,
talking for the entire drive, and later she would repeat
everything to her aunt and listen to the village gossip…

Lights twinkled ahead, and Uncle Bob slowed as
they passed the first of the row of houses and cottages
facing the loch, the rest of the village sprawling behind them. They drove past the hotel and on to the
end of the houses to her uncle's house, standing a
little apart—a solid square house with a cluster of
chimney pots at each end of its low roof, windows on
each side of its solid door, a row of windows above
them and two dormer windows higher still.

All the houses opened directly onto the narrow
road, but on its other side there was grass bordering
the rough beach of the loch. There were sheep wandering around but there was no sign of a human being.
Most people kept early nights and got up early, and
the few holidaymakers did the same, for there was
nowhere to go—no cinema or amusement arcade, no
parades of shops. The television was a blessing during
the winter, but those who lived there—fishermen, a
handful of commuters and retired folk—were perfectly content.

Aunt Kitty had the door open before they were out
of the Land Rover. She was a tall, thin woman with
a still handsome face, and grey hair swept into an old-
fashioned bun. She had been a good deal older than
Louisa's mother, and Louisa remembered her as a
very elegant and well-dressed woman. She still was,
but since her marriage fifteen years ago to Uncle Bob,
when she had been in her late forties, the elegance
had been transferred to tweeds, cashmere and stout

shoes—a countrywoman's wardrobe. She hugged Louisa with warmth.

'Prettier than ever! Lovely to see you again; you must be tired. Come on in, love. There's a meal waiting, and then off to bed with you.'

Louisa said, 'Oh, Aunt Kitty, this is heavenly. It's like another world—and I'm famished.'

She always had the same room when she came, the one overlooking the loch, with its old-fashioned bed, its patchwork quilt and the little basket chair by the window. There was a solid wardrobe and a washbasin in one corner, a small table by the bed and a handful of books on the ledge under the window.

They had been there since Louisa had first visited her aunt and uncle with her mother and father. She had been a teenager, and she had never forgotten how happy she had been. Her mother had died the following year and for a year or two she hadn't come, then she and her father had come again each year until he'd married Felicity, who had refused to return the visit Louisa's aunt and uncle had paid them soon after their marriage. So Louisa had begun to come on her own— not every year, but whenever she could.

She unpacked her case, ate a huge supper and went to bed, with the window wide to the night summer air, waking early to hang out of the window and watch the waters of the loch change colour as the sun rose.

Every time she came she was surprised afresh at the amount of things there were to do each day— rowing her uncle out into the loch so that he might fish, pottering in the garden behind the house, grubbing up weeds, digging potatoes. Driving to Torridon a few miles away so that her aunt could shop. And in the afternoons, while her uncle snoozed behind his newspaper and her aunt dozed over her knitting,

Louisa took herself off, behind the village, up into the hills which led across rugged country to the mountains, and sometimes, greatly daring, she rowed herself over to the small island in the loch.

It belonged to the Scottish National Trust, and there was a fairly constant stream of visitors, which, now the summer was advanced, was increasing, but now only a handful of people were there. It was quiet save for birds and wildlife, and Louisa lay on the grass, bare-legged and barefoot, wearing a wide cotton skirt and a thin cotton T-shirt, listening to the small noises she never heard in Salisbury—bees, dragonflies, birdsong, sheep bleating behind the village, the rustle of some small animal making its way through the undergrowth. A day for dreaming.

Half-awake, Louisa said, 'I wish Thomas was here...'

Thomas, after a morning being briefed by Sir James, had returned to his home. He had an evening surgery, but before that he had a good deal of paperwork to deal with. So he wasn't best pleased when Helena walked into his study.

He hadn't seen her over the weekend; she had been away visiting friends, and no amount of cajoling on her part had tempted him to go with her.

He had said, rather sternly, 'You don't understand, Helena. I'm a working man; I can't ignore that.'

She had been peevish about it. 'You could get a full-time secretary,' she told him, 'and another partner.'

She pouted prettily now. 'We've been asked to dine with Percy Witherspoon—tomorrow evening. I thought I'd let you know so that you would be free...'

'I'm afraid that it's not possible. I'm going to

Scotland in the morning. Sir James isn't able to attend
a seminar and see a patient there. I shall be gone for
several days—a week at least.'

Helena said furiously, 'Why didn't you tell me?
Someone else can go.'

'I'm afraid not. And I would have told you, Helena,
but you were away, and when I phoned I was told
you had gone for a drive with Witherspoon.'

She had the grace to look uncomfortable. 'At least
he bothers about me. What do you expect me to do?
Stay at home waiting for you to spend an hour or so
with me when you feel like it?'

'No, of course not. But, Helena, you must realise
that my work isn't a nine-to-five job.'

'Well, of course I do, but I thought you'd change
once we were engaged.' She added, 'I ought to be
more important to you than your work.'

When he didn't answer that, she said, 'I intend to
dine with Percy. Perhaps when you come back you'll
realise that I won't be second best, and give up some
of your stupid patients and enjoy life.'

'I'm sorry you feel like that,' Thomas was trying
to be fair, to see her point of view.

'Then do something about it.' Helena turned on her
heel, on her way out aiming a kick at Bellow, who
had risen politely to accompany her to the door. 'And
the first thing I do when we are married,' said Helena
furiously, 'will be to have this silly dog put down.'

She slammed the door after her, and Bellow pottered back to sit under Thomas's desk, looking hurt.

'Don't worry,' said Thomas. 'I'll never allow that,
old fellow.' He bent and studied his work again, but
presently raised his head to say, 'You shall come with
me to Scotland, Bellow. Rosie can get that niece of
hers to sleep here and keep her company.'

Bellow's tail thumped steadily in approval; he didn't like Helena.

They left very early in the morning, and Rosie, with Lucky the kitten tucked under her arm, watched them go. She gave a final wave as the car turned the corner and went back indoors.

'We'll miss him,' she told the kitten, 'but a few days away will do him the power of good and give him a rest from that woman. And, if she comes round here giving me orders, she'll get short shrift, I can tell you.'

Thomas had a long journey ahead of him, almost six hundred miles. He crossed country, picked up the M5 just north of Bristol and drove steadily north, merging presently with the M6. It was monotonous on the motorway but the car was warm and comfortable, and Bellow, sitting beside him, was a good companion. True, he had nothing to say, but he listened to every word Thomas uttered.

The doctor drove fast, sitting relaxed behind the wheel, stopping from time to time for a meal and to let Bellow browse, but he made good time and crossed over the border into Scotland in the late afternoon. By evening he was in Glasgow, comfortably installed in the house of one of Sir James's friends, a pleasant, elderly man with a charming wife. They made him very welcome, and Bellow, aware that he was welcome too, behaved impeccably.

Over dinner they discussed the following day's seminar. 'There will be a dinner in the evening,' Thomas was warned. 'Black tie and wives.'

'I do have a black tie with me,' said Thomas, 'but no wife, I'm afraid.'

'You're intending to marry, so James told me. You must come again and bring her with you.'

The next day was fully occupied, which was just as well, for it meant he had no time to think about Louisa. Only that night he allowed himself to dream a little. A dangerous thing to do, he knew, but it was all he had—dreams. Perhaps when he saw her again, talked to her, spent a few hours in her company he would be rid of this infatuation...

He went to Edinburgh in the morning and saw Professor Lutvik, who promised to go to Salisbury to discuss his theories with Sir James, and then in the late afternoon he drove on north to a small village just outside Inverness.

The house was large, secure behind high walls, and had a gate controlled by a gatekeeper. The drive was long, and the doctor stopped again as he neared the house. But he was expected, and presently was ushered into a vast hall by a butler, led into a small room, splendidly furnished, and asked to wait. The two young men who came eventually were friendly.

'You are not tired? You will be shown to your room, and please ask for anything you want. If you would conduct your examination tomorrow morning?'

'Certainly. I have my dog with me...'

'No trouble. There is a sitting room beside your bedroom with a balcony, and please feel free to walk in the grounds. We have guard dogs out overnight but they are shut up at seven o'clock each morning.'

The elder of the two men said, 'We look forward to dining with you at eight o'clock. Breakfast will be served to you in your sitting room.'

They smiled at him, their dark eyes twinkling. 'We hope that your report will be a good one, for we would wish to return to our own country.'

'Yes, of course. I'll phone Sir James and make sure

that he shares my opinion and let you know as soon as possible.'

They left him and he went out to his car to fetch Bellow. After a stroll round the grounds the pair of them went to his room, led there by the butler. Thomas was a little amused at the formality and signs of security, but was aware that the latter were necessary.

He dined presently with the two young men, went to bed early, and was up soon after seven o'clock to walk in the grounds with Bellow. It was going to be another glorious day, and driving across to Shieldaig would be a delight. And he would see Louisa—perhaps not today, but certainly tomorrow. He went in to his breakfast then, had a long talk with Sir James on the phone, and then went to sit on the balcony with Bellow until he was summoned to his patient.

The examination was a lengthy business, followed by a long talk with his patient, an even longer discussion on the phone with Sir James and finally a decision made that his patient might return to his own country, fully restored to health. It all took some time, so it was late afternoon by the time Thomas, with the faithful Bellow beside him, drove away, too late to arrive unannounced at Shieldaig. But Torridon was a mere sixty miles from Inverness. He drove there, not hurrying along the narrow road, and when he reached the town booked in at the Loch Torridon Hotel, a large house which had once been a shooting lodge. It stood in spacious grounds beside the loch and its luxurious comfort, after the grandeur of his patient's home, was a welcome surprise. The doctor, his mission accomplished, took Bellow for a long walk, ate a good dinner and went to his bed.

*   *   *

Louisa, a bare few miles away, went to bed early, too. She had been out on the loch for most of the day with her uncle, plying the oars while he fished. A delightful way to spend a day, but she had promised her aunt that she would pick the strawberries ready for jam-making in the morning, and all that rowing had tired her. She curled up in her bed with a contented sigh, allowed her thoughts to dwell briefly on Thomas, and went to sleep.

The weather had held. Everyone said they hadn't had such a lovely summer for years, and several of the older people in the village predicted that once the weather broke there would be nothing but wind and rain, and, later, snow. Aunt Kitty, who never listened to any weather forecasts, had great faith in the local inhabitants' opinions. The strawberries must be picked before the rain they forecast came.

Louisa had breakfast and, armed with a large bas-ket, went to the edge of the garden where it merged into the surrounding moorland and where her uncle had a large strawberry patch. She got down onto her knees and began picking. It was awkward work, but she enjoyed it. Just for the time being she was content. Salisbury seemed like another world. Her work, the patients, Sir James, Felicity and Percy, the odious Helena—they were jumbled up in a vague muddle she had thrust to the back of her head. Only Thomas had refused to join them there.

'Which is ridiculous,' said Louisa, talking to herself as she so often did, 'since it really doesn't matter if I never see him again. Only I hope he'll be happy...'

She took the first full basket to the kitchen, assured her aunt that she was enjoying herself, and went back to fill the second basket. There was no sign of the rain forecast in the village, but, said Aunt Kitty, 'Better to be safe than sorry.' And, 'When you've filled that basket there'll be coffee waiting for you and a slice of bannock.'

Aunt Kitty was sitting in the porch, stringing beans, when the doctor brought the Bentley to a quiet halt. She watched him get out of the car and come towards her. She wished him good morning, and added, 'You've come to see Louisa?'

'Good morning. Yes, indeed I have. Is she expecting me?'

'Gracious me, no. Never breathed a word about you coming here. Come on inside. She's picking strawberries, but she'll be back any minute now. Shall I call her?'

'I'd rather you didn't...'

'Come in, then. She's down at the end of the garden. I dare say you could do with a cup of coffee.' Aunt Kitty turned to look at him. 'You'll be the doctor—she mentioned you just the once. You've come a long way.' She stared up at his calm face and liked what she saw. He was the reason for Louisa's dreaminess when she thought no one was looking.

Aunt Kitty, scenting romance, sat him down in the kitchen and arranged the coffee cups. Five minutes later Louisa came in, her basket loaded, strawberry stains down the front of her cotton dress and round her mouth, her hair tied back with a ribbon, her delightful nose sprinkled with freckles.

Thomas, getting to his feet, thought he had never seen anyone as beautiful in his life and knew that this wasn't infatuation, this was love.

CHAPTER SEVEN

LOUISA put the basket down slowly, and stood staring at him. She said in a small, squeaky voice, 'Thomas?' And then, 'You're here…'

A stupid remark to make. She wished that she could think of something witty and amusing to say; she wished even more that she didn't look such a fright.

Thomas, watching her face, guessed what she was thinking. He said, carefully casual, 'Sir James had several appointments in Scotland and he felt that he couldn't leave his wife, so I'm deputising for him.'

'Oh, I see. Are you on your way back, then?'

'Er, no. I still have a few days before I return. I remembered that you were here at Shieldaig and hoped you would show me some of the country around here.'

'A sensible idea,' said Aunt Kitty. 'Go and wash your face, Louisa. We'll have coffee and you can take the doctor a bit of the way up Ben Shieldaig. It'll give you both an appetite for lunch.' She looked at the doctor. 'You'll come here, of course. Staying at the hotel, are you?'

He smiled and said yes.

'They'll look after you very well, but come and go here as you wish. I shall call you Thomas.' She turned to look at Louisa, who was still hovering by the door.

'Run along, child, what's keeping you? No need to fuss about your clothes; there's no one to see you— nor your hair.'

Louisa went up to her room then. Did her aunt sup-

129

pose that Thomas was blind? She must change her
stained dress and put up her hair. And halfway
through doing that she paused to wonder if it mattered. He never looked at her—not to see her—only
that once when she had told him about it. All the
same, she got into a denim skirt and a cotton top and
pinned her hair in a ferocious bundle on the top of
her head.

And Thomas, not blind at all, thought she looked
even more beautiful when she went back downstairs.

Aunt Kitty gave them coffee and bannock and
urged them out of the house. 'One o'clock sharp,' she
reminded them. 'Your uncle will be back and want
his lunch.' She added, 'Enjoy yourselves!'

Louisa, leading the way across the rough grass towards the lower slopes of Ben Shieldaig, thought that
would be unlikely. She couldn't think why Thomas
had come and, being Louisa, not given to mincing her
words, she said so.

Thomas was ready for that. 'The other two appointments aren't until the end of next week, so I have
time on my hands.'

He told her this so convincingly that she didn't
doubt him. 'Oh, well,' said Louisa, aware of regret
that he hadn't come to see her for any other reason
than that of filling in the waiting days. She added
lamely, 'There are some splendid walks here.'

'Good. You must show them to me.'

They were beginning to climb the first gentle
slopes. 'You're not going to stay here?'

Louisa speaking her mind again, reflected the doctor, and he said easily, 'Well, I have had quite a lot
of driving; I could do with a couple of days using my
legs instead of the car. Besides, Bellow needs a good
run...'

'Bellow? He's here? With you? Where is he, then?' She had stopped, looking anxious.

'He's at the hotel. Quite happy, I assure you. He had a good walk this morning and now he's resting his elderly bones on my bed. Tomorrow we'll have a ramble along the loch—take sandwiches.' He added with just the right amount of casualness, 'Come with us, if you like; he'll be delighted to see you again.'

'Well, yes, I'd like to see him, too. And Lucky— how is he? Will he really grow into a fine cat?'

He smiled. 'Perhaps not as fine as Dr Johnson's Hodge, but he's doing his best.'

He glanced sideways at Louisa, walking beside him, matching her steps to his. Odds and ends of hair had broken free from her topknot, her cheeks were a healthy pink, her bare arms were faintly tanned and she was quite unconscious of her appearance. Helena, he reflected, would have worn an elegant sun hat to protect her make-up and a dress which needed care and attention, and she would have worn the kind of sandals which would have been useless on this rough grass. But then, Helena wouldn't have come in the first place, would she?

They climbed steadily and presently sat down to rest. The sun was warm now, the sky a brilliant blue, the water shining like glass.

'This is a magnificent place,' observed the doctor. 'Will you mind leaving it?'

'Yes. Each time I come I tell myself that I'll come again very soon, but somehow it isn't possible—although now that Felicity lives on her own and has so many friends she won't want me to go on holiday with her, so I'll come again. I'd like to come for Christmas.'

Louisa had stretched out on the grass. She had

kicked off her sandals and the gentle wind was playing havoc with her topknot. Her eyes were shut but she went on talking. 'Is it a secret your being up here? Something to do with Sir James going off like that in a hurry?'

'Partly a secret, so don't ask questions.'

'I've often wondered—do doctors tell their wives things they're not supposed to talk about?'

'I imagine it rather depends on the wife...'

She opened an eye to look at him. 'Will you tell Helena when you're married?'

'You have an unruly tongue, Louisa. I have no intention of answering that.'

The splendid air must have gone to Louisa's head; she said airily, 'Oh, have I annoyed you? I expect you're wishing that she was here instead of me.'

The doctor, who wasn't wishing anything of the sort, merely grunted.

She sat up and put on her sandals again. She said, 'It's hard for us to be friends, isn't it? Now and then we get on quite well, don't we? And then I say something you don't approve of and you come over all distant. We'd better go back; it'll be lunch time by the time we get there.' She hesitated. 'If you'd rather not stay for lunch... There's nothing worse than having to eat a meal with someone you don't see eye to eye with.'

The doctor said in a quiet voice, 'Perhaps we might bury the hatchet? Just for a few days while I am in Scotland?'

'Well, that would be nice. We could forget about the consulting rooms and Percy and Helena.'

He got up and pulled her to her feet. 'We'll shake on that.' As they started back he asked, 'Have your aunt and uncle always lived here?'

She explained about them as they strolled back. 'Aunt Kitty is my mother's elder sister. She didn't marry until she was in her forties. Uncle Bob has lived here for years; the house was his father's, and his grandfather's before him. He's retired now, but he had a solicitor's practice in Torridon. They're two of the happiest and most contented people I know.'

'They are to be envied. Your aunt lived in Salisbury before she married?'

'No, she was a fashion buyer for a big shop in Bath; she used to come and see mother when she was alive.'

'This is a far cry from a fashion showroom.'

'She hasn't missed it. I think that's because she loves Uncle Bob so much, nothing else is as important.'

'She is to be envied, and so is your uncle—to have such a wife must be something every man longs for.'

Louisa, on the point of making some polite remark about Helena, decided against it. He had spoken casually but the look on his face was bleak.

Uncle Bob was home for lunch; it was a leisurely meal, and he and his guest discovered a mutual interest in trout fishing, although they were polite enough to include Aunt Kitty and Louisa in their talk. It was early afternoon before Thomas got up to go, but only after he had suggested that Louisa might like to show him more of the country round the loch.

'We might take Bellow and find a pub for lunch?'

He was just sufficiently casual, and at the same time too friendly to refuse. Besides, Louisa didn't want to refuse. She said, 'All right, but I'll bring some sandwiches.'

'Splendid. About ten o'clock?'

After he had gone, Aunt Kitty said briskly, 'Well,

there's a decent man for you. He must be a splendid doctor, one you can trust.'

Louisa said primly, 'Yes, I believe he's very well thought of. I don't know much about him.' She added, 'He's engaged to a beautiful girl,' just so that Aunt Kitty didn't get ideas into her head.

Her aunt gave her an innocent look. 'That doesn't surprise me. Will they marry soon?'

'I don't know. They—he never talks about it.'

'You would think that a handsome, successful man, engaged to a beautiful girl, would want to marry without delay. Perhaps he hasn't a house?'

'He has a lovely house—in a very small village— old and rambling and beautifully furnished.'

'Oh, well,' said Aunt Kitty, getting to the root of the matter. 'The girl is in no hurry to wed.'

'She is having too good a time and…' She paused. 'She is so sure of him that she will only marry when she wants to. Her name is Helena and she is the most unsuitable wife for Thomas. I hate her!'

Aunt Kitty, satisfied with her probing, said comfortably, 'She sounds perfectly horrid. Men can be so stupid, you know, when it comes to their own feelings.'

They were lucky with the weather. It was a glorious day again. With food and drink in a rucksack on the doctor's shoulders, and Bellow prancing around them, they set off. They walked miles, stopping to admire the view from time to time, eating their sandwiches sitting on an outcrop of rock above the loch, talking about nothing in particular.

They got back in time for tea at Aunt Kitty's— scones and honey, bannock, baps with strawberry jam, sponge cake light as air, and endless cups of tea.

Louisa, listening to Thomas and Uncle Bob discussing sheep farming, wished that the day would
never end. But, of course, it did. The doctor went
away presently, saying all the right things with his
beautiful manners to her aunt, and adding casually,
'A very pleasant day, Louisa. I shall be away tomorrow and part of the day following. And then I have
Sir James's appointments. You return on Saturday,
don't you? So do I. I'll drive you back.'

He watched her face carefully as he spoke and saw
disappointment, chased away by hastily assumed in-
difference.

'That's very kind of you, but I have my return train
ticket.'

'You can trade that in when you get back. We'll
leave here mid-morning, spend the night on the way
and get back to Salisbury the following evening.'

'Where?' asked Louisa.

'The Lakes. I told my mother to expect us.'

'But I haven't said I'll come with you...and I don't
know your mother.'

'A good opportunity to get to know each other,' he
said cheerfully.

Most unfairly, she thought, he enlisted Aunt Kitty's
aid. 'Don't you think it is a good idea?' he wanted to
know.

'Very sensible. So much pleasanter than that long
train journey and getting back tired out. Especially
since you have to work in the morning, Louisa.'

'Well,' said Louisa slowly, 'if I won't be in the
way at your home, I'll come with you.' She gave him
a sharp look to make sure that he wasn't being polite.
There was nothing but friendliness in his face, and
she had to admit to herself that she enjoyed his company, although probably once they were back in

Salisbury they would resume their guarded attitude towards each other.

'Splendid,' said Thomas. 'I'll pick you up around ten o'clock on Saturday morning.'

'You'll have coffee before you go?' asked Aunt Kitty. 'And you'll take a pot of my strawberry jam to your mother...'

Louisa had to admit to feeling lonely when he had gone. It's only because there's no one else and it was pleasant to have someone to walk with, she reflected, and I dare say he felt the same, since he had to be here anyway. She wondered if he would tell Helena, and decided that he would; he wasn't a man to conceal anything from his future wife. Helena wasn't going to like it, though.

Louisa thought of her efforts to get Percy and Helena interested in each other and wished that she had never meddled. It was none of her business whom Thomas married; probably Helena loved him dearly, and as for him, although he had never shown his feelings in public, he must be wildly in love with her. The very idea made her feel so wretched that she went for a long and tiring walk in the sudden rain, assuring her aunt that she simply had to see as much of the loch as she could before she went home again.

But it gave her the opportunity to think clearly. When she got back she would try and undo any harm which she might have done—perhaps coerce Percy back to herself, much though she disliked the idea, and leave the doctor and Helena to be together as often as possible. If she could persuade Percy to spend as much time as possible with her, then probably he and Helena would presently become less interested in each other.

Filled with uplifting thoughts, Louisa went to bed.

On Saturday, her bags packed, once more in the suitable outfit for travelling and her hair pinned securely, Louisa went downstairs to wish Thomas a good morning.

He was standing by the open kitchen door, talking to her uncle, but he turned to look at her. A long look which took in her formal clothes and disciplined hair; already she was well on the way to being Miss Howarth again. She looked a little pale, too, and worried, and he wondered why. Perhaps because she was sad at leaving. He said cheerfully that it was going to be a lovely day and driving to the Lakes would be delightful.

A remark to which she replied politely as she drank her coffee. Not the happy, carefree girl who had walked the hills with him, thought the doctor, but whether she was Miss Howarth or Louisa he wasn't able to forget her for one moment. And, even if she didn't return his love, he knew that he could never marry Helena. And, even though the prospect didn't look too good, he had every intention of marrying Louisa.

They set off presently, waved away with warm invitations to return as soon as they could, Aunt Kitty blithely taking it for granted that they would come together. Louisa, her head twisted round to look back so that she could get a last glimpse of the house and the village, and finally a last glimpse, too, of the loch, faced front at last and stared ahead of her. She wanted to weep because she had been happy and because she wasn't sure what awaited her when they reached Salisbury.

'We'll go as far as Spean Bridge and then on to

Fort William. We'll stop there for lunch, then take the A82, go through the Pass of Glencoe and Rannoch Moor to Glasgow, then go down the A74 to Carlisle. We can stop for tea before we cross over into England.'

He spoke casually, not looking at her, making light of their long journey.

'Where do we go from Carlisle?'

'Troutbeck. A village about thirty miles from Carlisle, a few miles north of Windermere. It's very small, buried in the hills.'

'It's your family home?'

'Yes. My mother lives there. Are you quite comfortable? Is Bellow asleep?'

She turned to look. 'Yes. Does he like long journeys?'

'Oh, yes. He's gone everywhere with me since he was a puppy.'

He began to tell her about Lucky, keeping up a gentle flow of talk, and the awkwardness she had been feeling gradually slipped away. So silly, she thought; she had never felt awkward with him before. Even when they hadn't been the best of friends she had never felt uncertain and—horrors—shy of him. Realising that made her stiff and reserved again, although Thomas didn't appear to notice, pointing out interesting bits of scenery as they sped past, for all the world as though he was thoroughly enjoying himself.

Which he was, of course.

At Fort William he took her to one of the hotels, left her to find the Ladies, told her he would meet her in the bar, and went for a brisk walk with Bellow. Louisa, tidying her already tidy hair and powdering her freckled nose, took a good look at herself. She had a healthy colour from all the fresh air at her aunt's house, but she didn't look her best somehow. She practised a few smiles and cheerful expressions, decided that she had got fat, and, thoroughly dissatisfied with her person, went along to the bar.

Thomas and Bellow were already there, sitting at a table overlooking the street, and they both got to their feet as she reached them. Bellow greeted her as though he hadn't seen her for weeks, but the doctor was more restrained.

'We'll eat here, if you don't mind. Sandwiches? A salad? I'd like to get on again as soon as possible. What would you like to drink?'

'Tonic and lemon, thanks, and sandwiches will be fine. I had a huge breakfast. I must stop eating for a bit—all that good wholesome Highland food...'

When he'd given their order he gave her a leisurely glance. 'You're just right as you are.'

She cast him a suspicious look. He was being polite, not meaning a word of it, otherwise how could he be in love with Helena and her complete lack of curves?

He was watching her face. 'No, I mean it, Louisa.' He was smiling a little, and she blushed and then frowned fiercely, annoyed with herself because of it. The arrival of the sandwiches caused a welcome diversion.

They were off again very shortly, driving down the A82 towards Glasgow, still miles away. The Bentley was comfortable and roomy and there was little traffic, the scenery was beautiful, grand and awe-inspiring under a blue sky. 'I could go on for ever,' said Louisa suddenly.

'So could I, but probably for a different reason.'

He sounded as though he was laughing. 'We're making good time; I had expected more traffic.'

They had crossed Rannoch Moor and presently were driving alongside Loch Lomond. For almost sixty miles there was a series of unending beauty until they neared Glasgow. Thomas worked his way round the edge of the city and picked up the motorway to Carlisle. At Gretna, he cut across to the A74.

'Tea?' he asked. 'You must be longing for a cup. We'll stop in the next village.'

They stopped at Blackford, just north of Carlisle, for their tea, a splendid meal of teacakes, scones, bannock, and a dish of pastries rich with cream.

'This is my final fling,' said Louisa, choosing a second cake. 'I shall eat nothing but salads and those horrid biscuit things which taste like hay.'

Before they reached Carlisle, the doctor joined the M6, and at Penrith took the road to Troutbeck, still another twenty-five miles or so. Louisa stared out at the distant mountains and felt nervous. Supposing his mother didn't like her? And would she wonder why he hadn't brought Helena with him instead of a complete stranger? The doctor hadn't spoken for some time, and she wondered uneasily if he was regretting his invitation.

They were on a narrow country road now, surrounded by wooded hills and wide meadows. There was no sign of a village, only an occasional farmhouse standing well back from the road.

Louisa said, 'Are we nearly there? It's very beautiful country.'

There was no need for him to answer for round the next bend she saw the first of the houses. Troutbeck was a scattered village, strung out along the road for the best part of a mile, a charming mixture of cottages, small, neat houses which looked as though they had been there for ever, and larger houses on the lower slopes of the hills behind them.

At the very end of the village the doctor turned into a narrow side lane and then through an open gateway, along a short drive bordered by shrubs, and stopped before the door of the house at its end. A house built of grey stone, ample in size and with a wing to one side. It had tall chimneys and a large conservatory along one wall. There were trees around it, and a vast lawn like green velvet surrounded by flowerbeds.

'How very nice,' said Louisa, getting out of the car as the doctor held the door for her. She looked at him and smiled. 'That's quite inadequate, isn't it? Did you grow up here?'

'I was born here. It's been in the family for a very long time. Come in and meet my mother!'

He whistled to Bellow and they crossed the raked gravel and went through the open door into a wide hall with a curving staircase at its end. There were a great many doors, and one of them was flung open now and his mother came towards them.

'Thomas, my dear.' She lifted her face for his kiss, and Louisa had a moment to study her hostess. As tall as herself, rather stout, elegantly dressed with grey hair worn in an old-fashioned style. Mrs Gifford must have been a very pretty woman in her youth. Indeed, she was still remarkably handsome...

'Mother, this is Louisa Howarth.' He looked at Louisa and smiled. 'Louisa, this is my mother.'

Louisa took the hand offered to her and met the blue eyes squarely. They were just like her son's— clear and sharp.

'We shall like each other,' said Mrs Gifford rather disconcertingly. 'Come and see your room and then

we'll dine. You must be hungry; you've come a long
way. Thomas, bring the bags in, will you? I've put
Louisa in the little summer room.'

Another door opened and a stout, elderly little
woman trotted towards them. 'Mr Thomas, there you
are at last.' A beady dark eye took in Louisa. 'And
your young lady.' She lifted a round, wrinkled face
for him to kiss. 'And just you leave those bags for
me...'

The doctor hugged her. 'Ada, you grow more beautiful each time I see you. Leave the bags. This is Miss
Louisa Howarth—doubtless you know all about her.'

Ada bounced over to Louisa. 'And as pretty a picture as ever I did see.' She pronounced, 'You'll be a
bonny bride, miss; I'll be glad to dance at your wedding.'

Louisa opened her mouth to explain and caught
Mrs Gifford's eye. 'I'll explain later,' said that lady
sotto voce and led the way up the uncarpeted staircase.

'I do apologise for that, Louisa—I may call you
that? Ada has been with us since she was a young
girl—she's part of the family. She's getting old now,
but she still acts as our housekeeper, although she has
plenty of help. But she does get confused at times,
especially when she gets excited. She adores Thomas,
you see, and I fancy she thinks you are to marry him.'

Mrs Gifford had paused on the wide landing, and
they stood facing each other.

'But she must have met Helena?'

Mrs Gifford didn't smile. 'Helena has never been
here. It seems she dislikes this part of England...'

'Oh, dear,' said Louisa. 'But I expect she'll change
her mind once they're married. I do hope so. It's such
a glorious bit of England.'

She added after a moment, 'But it's beautiful

around Salisbury, too. Thomas has a lovely house. I had to go there and help him a bit while Sir James was away.'

Mrs Gifford, who knew all about that, asked, 'You live in Salisbury? Such a lovely cathedral…'

They wandered slowly along the landing, and now she stopped by one of the doors. 'Here is your room, my dear. I hope you will be comfortable. If you want anything, do please ask me.'

They smiled at each other, liking each other, knowing that they could be friends.

'I'm sure I shall be very comfortable,' said Louisa. 'It was very kind of you to invite me.' She added, 'And kind of Thomas to give me a lift.'

'I dare say driving is less tiring than the train, besides you can stop when you want to.'

Louisa agreed, thinking that more frequent stops would have been welcome.

They went into the room together. Such a pretty room, too, the bed having a headboard of some pale wood which matched the dressing table under the window and the tallboy against one wall. Fragile little tables were on each side of the bed, bearing pink-shaded lamps, and the coverlet matched the pastel chintz curtains. The whole effect was of a casual mix of pastels, doubtless carefully thought out. There was a bathroom beyond, and a carpet in which one could sink one's feet.

'Oh,' said Louise. 'What a lovely place in which to fall asleep and wake up.'

Mrs Gifford smiled. 'I'm glad you like it. The house is old, you know, and we take great care of it. When Thomas marries he will come and live here. Perhaps not for a few years, but he will want his children to come here and learn to love it, too.'

Helena, reflected Louisa, would have to change her ways considerably.

'Come down when you're ready,' said Mrs Gifford, and she went away. Louisa set about repairing the ravages of their long drive. It would have to be the same outfit but it was a garment which adapted itself to almost any occasion. She did her face, her hair and then went downstairs.

As she reached the hall the doctor flung open a door.

'In here, Louisa; come and have a drink before supper.'

The drawing room was large, with windows overlooking the garden, and a door opened onto a wide veranda. It was furnished very much as it had been for years, Louisa supposed, a charming mixture of Georgian cabinets, rent tables, and a magnificent longcase clock. Mingled in with these were some great armchairs, a couple of little crinoline chairs and on either side of the fireplace two sofas with a low table between them.

Bellow was there, sitting by his master's chair, and on the other side of the hearth was a basket. There were two cats curled up together asleep in it. A rather grand room, but lived-in. Louisa sipped her sherry and felt at home. If she had the chance, she promised herself, she would take a look at the portraits on the walls, and there was a splendid painting over the fireplace; it looked like a Landseer...

They ate their supper presently in another very large room—rather sombre by reason of the dark oak furniture and the heavy red brocade curtains, but the table gleamed with silver and crystal, and there was a bowl of sweet-scented roses at its centre.

Louisa, hungry after their journey, polished off the

watercress soup, the salmon, new potatoes and salad
and found room for the apple tart and cream which
followed them. And while they ate they talked—gossip from the village, their pleasant days at Shieldaig,
the majestic scenery they had travelled through that
day. But never a word about Helena.

They had their coffee in the drawing room, and
Louisa excused herself with the plea of tiredness and
took herself off to bed. Mother and son would have
a great deal to talk about, she had no doubt. But she
wasn't as tired as all that. She pottered about, spent a
long time in the bath, and then went to look out of
the window. It was a clear night with a bright moon,
and she could see the garden clearly. It would be nice
to explore it, but there wouldn't be time in the morning.

She was turning away when she saw Thomas with
Bellow; he was strolling along, his hands in his pockets. He had his back to the house, but suddenly he
stopped, turned round and looked up. She felt sure
that he hadn't seen her, but all the same she shot away
from the window and tumbled into bed and, since she
was tired now, she went to sleep at once, without
bothering to wonder why she had felt suddenly shy at
the idea of him seeing her.

Drinking her early-morning tea, she was aware of
cheerful sounds in the house. Bellow barking, cheerful
voices, quiet movements in the house, and presently
a thundering thump on her door.

'Come on down and take a walk round the garden,'
Thomas invited through the door. 'Breakfast in half
an hour, so be quick.'

She needed no second bidding. She showered and
dressed without bothering much about her face or hair

and nipped downstairs. The doctor was in the hall
with the door wide open behind him and Bellow on
the step. His 'Good morning' was affable. 'Slept
well?' he wanted to know. 'A pity that we can't spend
a few days here. I must try and get back before the
summer is over...'

Some imp in Louisa's head caused her to say, 'And
bring Helena with you.'

They had started to cross the lawn, and he came to
a halt to look down at her. 'Now, why should you say
that?' he wanted to know mildly.

Louisa went pink. 'Oh, I don't know. Well, yes, I
do know, really. If—I mean, *when* you marry, this
will be her home for some of the time, won't it? She
must surely want to see it.' She said earnestly, remembering guiltily about Percy, 'You really should
bring her, you know.'

He said evenly, 'When I need advice about my private life, Louisa, I will ask you for it.'

Looking up at him, she saw how cold his eyes
were, belying the quietness of his voice. He didn't like
her; all this time he had hidden his dislike with an
easygoing, pleasant manner and she had thought that
they were friends...

She said coolly, 'I'm not going to apologise. I
thought that I could say what I thought to you—
friends do, you know. But we aren't friends, are we?
If you would prefer it, you can take me to Kendal and
I'll get a train.'

'I shall drive you back to your flat, Louisa.' He
began to walk on. 'Would you like to see the rose
garden? We are rather proud of it...'

So a veil was to be drawn over the awkward epi-
sode, thought Louisa, at least while she was a guest
in his house. She admired the roses and presently they

returned to the house and joined his mother for breakfast, and she was careful to make cheerful conversation. It was fortunate that she had seen the rose garden, for it made a good topic of conversation.

They left shortly after breakfast. Ada bade them a rather tearful goodbye and, still uncertain as to who Louisa really was, bade her to come again soon.

Mrs Gifford didn't say that. 'I'm quite sure we shall see each other again,' she observed, 'and I shall look forward to that.'

It seemed most unlikely, but Louisa murmured politely and, invited to kiss a nicely made-up cheek, did so and then wandered away so that mother and son could say their goodbyes.

Mrs Gifford lifted her face for her son's kiss. 'You've quarrelled,' she said.

'Hardly that, Mother.' He smiled suddenly. 'You like Louisa, don't you?'

'Yes, dear. Drive carefully, and do remember that the poor girl might like to stop from time to time.' She put up a hand to touch his cheek. 'Come again soon, Thomas.'

She watched them drive away with Ada beside her.

'She'll make him a good wife,' said Ada as they went back into the house.

'Yes, Ada, she will, although neither of them know that at the moment.' Ada, who was getting deaf, didn't hear her.

They took the road to Kendal through lovely country, and once through the town joined the M6. Louisa had hoped that they might drive back along the lesser roads but a side glance at the doctor's stern profile stopped her from saying anything. No doubt he felt

that the quicker they got back, the sooner he would
be rid of her.

Once on the motorway, the countryside more or
less hidden, she had the leisure to think. Beyond asking her if she was comfortable, Thomas had little to
say to her, and she told herself that she didn't care,
that although he didn't deserve it she would do her
best to prise Percy away from Helena. Of course, they
could have cooled off considerably during the two
weeks she had been away...

They stopped for coffee mid-morning at a service
station, bustling with people. Thomas told her to find
a table while he went for coffee, which was a lengthy
business, and the coffee was awful. Telling her that
he would be outside with Bellow and she could join
them when she was ready, he left her. He was atten-
tive to her wants and polite, but remote. Louisa made
the best of it, got back into the car and thanked him
for the coffee.

From time to time they made a remark about the
scenery or the weather, like two people unable to get
away from each other in a doctor's waiting room,
feeling they must be civil at all costs. It was a relief
when he turned off the motorway, drove a mile or
two into the country and stopped at a hotel in
Worfield.

'We will lunch here.' He smiled a little. 'After that
coffee, I owe you a decent meal.'

It was a pleasant place and the food was good. They
maintained a desultory talk over their meal, and
Louisa was careful to mind her tongue. That her companion was treating her with an icy civility which was
tiresome, to say the least of it, was something she
supposed she deserved.

They drove on again without loss of time, and since

it was a warm afternoon Louisa dozed off sometimes, lulled by the car's comfort and Bellow's gentle, whiskery muzzle pressed into the back of her neck. She was asleep when they left the motorway at last and began the cross-country drive to Salisbury. Indeed, they were on the A303, almost there, when she woke up. It was late afternoon now and she longed for a cup of tea; in half an hour or so she would be able to have it in her own little flat.

The doctor turned off the road into a narrow lane, and she sat up to ask, 'Is this a short cut? I thought Salisbury was the turning further on.'

'It is. We are stopping for tea. There's a decent hotel at Telfont Evias.'

'But isn't it too late for tea?'

He didn't reply but drew up at the hotel entrance— a charming old house with the church nearby. Bidding the patient Bellow to stay, they went inside to be welcomed by a friendly soul who wanted to know how she could help.

Ten minutes later Louisa was sitting on a terrace outside the dining room, a tray of tea on the table beside her. Thomas was taking Bellow for a walk and had told her to drink her tea and order more when he got back.

Sitting beside her presently, with a fed and watered Bellow back in the car, he told her that he had asked for a meal in half an hour or so. 'We can go for a stroll through the village,' he suggested. 'Unless you would rather stay here?'

She was glad to stretch her legs; there was time to look round the church, cast an eye over the village, which was charming, and then take Bellow back to the car again before they sat down to a meal—chicken salad and jacket potatoes, and raspberries and cream for pudding. It was almost dusk by the time they got into the car once more, and fifteen minutes later they stopped before her door.

Louisa made haste to get out, making a dignified speech of thanks as she did so. It was wasted, though, as Thomas had got out too and was opening her door.

He took her key, opened the flat door, carried her case and bag upstairs, wished her goodnight, kissed her hard and drove away.

CHAPTER EIGHT

LOUISA stood and looked at the closed door. After a day spent in his austere company, his kiss had come as a surprise. There had been nothing austere about it, and she could only assume that his thoughts had been filled by Helena and he had forgotten who he was with.

She moved presently to unpack, open the windows and put the kettle on, automatically doing the small chores needed before she could go to bed. He hadn't said that he would see her in the morning and she was thankful for that, because for some reason she felt shy at the thought of seeing him again.

She went to bed presently, her head full of muddled thoughts, but she was too tired to sort them out, and in the morning there was no time to ponder them.

Once back at her desk, there was enough work to keep her busy for several days. Besides that, even when she had a few minutes of leisure, Mrs Grant and Jilly wanted to know about her holiday. Even Sir James paused in the perusal of his appointment book to ask her if she had had a good time.

'Did you come across Dr Gifford?' he asked artlessly. 'He took over for me—those dates I had booked earlier on.'

Louisa said that, yes, she had met him, and then asked how Sir James's wife was.

'Better, better, I'm glad to say. Where did you meet in Scotland?'

There was no help for it. Louisa gave Sir James a pared-down version of Thomas's arrival at Shieldaig.

'Oh, very nice,' observed Sir James, and shot a look at her rather pale face. Louisa, who never looked downcast, had the air of someone who was unhappy and determined to hide it at all costs. A pity that Thomas was going to marry that Thornfold girl. Sir James had always considered Louisa to be a sensible girl, but perhaps a couple of days in Thomas's company had caused her to lose her heart? On the other hand, they might have disliked each other's company; there had never been any sign of friendliness when Thomas had been at the consulting rooms. He must remember to observe them when Thomas came again. A pity that wouldn't be for several days.

The doctor, back in his own home, didn't allow his thoughts to dwell on Louisa. In the morning he would be back at the surgery, and in the meantime there were phone calls to make, letters to read and, as though there wasn't enough to keep his thoughts from his own problems, a request from one of his partners to give his opinion on a small boy with suspected meningitis. So it was long past midnight when he finally got to his bed. Shieldaig and Louisa seemed like a dream, he thought tiredly, before he slept.

He was at the surgery by half past eight, ready to take over from the locum and spend the morning seeing patients before going out on his round. A far-flung one too, to remote farms miles away from anywhere, and a travellers' camp with several children with measles and an almost total lack of hygiene. He was glad to get home at last, to be met in the hall by Rosie.

'Miss Thornfold's in the drawing room, sir,' she

told him, po-faced. 'I've got Lucky and Bellow with me in the kitchen.'

Thomas's impassive features gave nothing away as to his feelings. He thanked Rosie and went into the drawing room. Helena was standing by the open door to the garden, a sight to gladden any man's heart, in a silky, swirly dress the colour of a summer sky, only she didn't gladden his.

'Helena—did Rosie give you tea? Would you like a drink?'

'So you're back. You said you'd only be away a week—you've made me look a fool...' Her pretty face was ugly with temper.

'I phoned you, but I was told you weren't available. I left a message. Did you not get it?'

She shrugged. 'Why so much time in Scotland, of all places?'

'Well, it was arranged rather hurriedly. Sir James's wife was ill and he didn't wish to leave her.' He went to stand beside her. 'You know, Helena, that my life is hardly my own. That is something you must get accustomed to if you marry me.'

Her eyes narrowed. Was he crying off? She had been so sure of him—a solid future, plenty of money, a pleasant lifestyle and, since he was so engrossed in his work, she would have all the freedom she wanted. She thought of Percy with a sudden pang. They had such fun together and they shared so many interests, but she wasn't sure if he outweighed the advantages Thomas had to offer.

She smiled with sudden brilliance. 'I don't mean to be horrid, darling. I missed you dreadfully. We must make up for it. When you can manage a few hours free we will go somewhere quiet where we can talk. We might even discuss a date for the wedding.'

Thomas looked down at the beautiful face smiling up at him.

'Helena, are you sure…?' He got no further because the phone rang.

Within minutes he was in his car, on his way to an accident on the Salisbury road, leaving Helena, white with temper, to get into her own car and drive herself home.

Her temper cooled presently; perhaps it was as well that he had been interrupted in whatever he had intended to say. She couldn't guess what it would have been, but she felt uneasy. Was he having second thoughts about their marriage? She had kept him dangling for a long time, and after the first few months hadn't pretended to have any interest in his work.

Forewarned was forearmed, she reflected. She knew she was beautiful and she knew, too, that she could be charming—and she knew how to attract men… Once safely married to Thomas there would be no harm in a little flirting. After all, life was going to be boring if she was supposed to stay home waiting for him each evening. She took a quick peek in the side mirror and smiled at her reflection.

The accident was a bad one. The doctor left his car in the care of the police and went with one of the injured men in the ambulance to Salisbury. He had a fractured spine, and any undue movement or jolting would cause his death. Thomas stayed at Odstock Hospital until the man had been taken to Theatre, and by then it was almost midnight. He got a porter to ring for a car and was driven back to where his own car was still parked by the side of the road. The police were still there, supervising the towing away of the wrecked cars, and he wished them goodnight and drove home again.

His house was in darkness save for a lamp in the hall, but Rosie was there waiting.

'There's soup ready, and you'd better have a drink…'

'I can't, Rosie, I'm on call, but the soup will be very welcome. You shouldn't have stayed up.'

'Well, someone has to look after you. Once you're married, your wife can do that.' She followed him into the kitchen and poured the soup into a pitkin. 'Miss Thornfold went home,' she told him in an expressionless voice.

The doctor stooped to pat Bellow and tickle Lucky's tiny chin. 'Well, yes, I didn't expect her to stay.'

Rosie gave a snorting 'huh'. 'I'm back to my bed, sir,' she said 'unless there's anything you want.'

'No, thanks, Rosie. It was good of you to stay up, and this soup is delicious.' He went to open the door for her. 'Goodnight.'

He was at the consulting rooms soon after nine o'clock the following morning for he had a good deal to discuss with Sir James. He wished Mrs Grant and Jilly good morning as he went through the waiting room, to find Louisa there, checking the appointments book with Sir James.

He bade her an unsmiling good morning and saw at a glance that she was Miss Howarth once more— not a hair out of place and wearing one of her elegant, unassuming outfits which turned her into a perfect receptionist. Her own good morning was composed as she slipped out of the room. She heard Sir James's hearty 'Thomas—good to see you back. Have you seen Helena? She must have missed you…'

The doctor said evenly that he had seen her briefly. 'But I got called away—that accident last night…'

'Ah, yes. Very nasty.' They exchanged medical details before Sir James said, 'Now, tell me about our patient. He's anxious to get home?'

Louisa was glad that she was occupied with a patient's queries when Thomas came back. She listened to his retreating footsteps and wanted most dreadfully to run after him while she smilingly assured the patient that her bill would be sent to her in due course. Thomas had looked tired; she didn't know that he had been out for a good part of the night, but she did wonder if he had seen Helena.

She bade a polite goodbye to the patient and reflected that she would go and see Felicity that evening and find out if Percy and Helena were still meeting and seeing each other. She had no wish to get on cordial terms with Percy again, but she couldn't bear to see Thomas look like that—a kind of stony calm which must mask heaven only knew what feelings.

She waited until she had had her supper before going to see Felicity, so that it was already faintly dusk when Biddy opened the door to her.

'A sight for sore eyes,' said Biddy. 'The missus is in the drawing room with Mr Witherspoon. I'll bring in some fresh coffee.' She looked at Louisa's face. 'Had a good holiday? I must say you look a bit peaky.'

'I had a lovely time. It's hot in the consulting rooms,' said Louisa, and made her way to the drawing room.

Her stepmother was lounging on a sofa, but she sat up as Louisa went in.

'Darling, how lovely to see you again. Did you have a good holiday in that God-forsaken place? The cards you sent look delightful, but I don't suppose they're anything like the real thing.'

'Oh, but they are,' said Louisa. 'Though the real thing's better.' She turned to greet Percy with a smile. 'Hello—we haven't seen each other for ages. How are you, Percy? What have you been doing with yourself?'

'Mending the poor heart you broke, Louisa.' He contrived to look downcast.

Louisa laughed. 'I'm sure you've found plenty of girls to mend it for you.' She raised enquiring brows so that it sounded like a question.

'I must admit that the blow was softened to a certain extent...'

'Helena Thornfold has been doing her best,' said Felicity. Her voice held an edge of spite.

'A marvellous girl,' said Percy. 'She isn't only beautiful, she shares so many of my opinions and ideas. We are never at a loss when we are together.'

Louisa said flatly, 'She's going to marry Dr Gifford.'

'I have tried to make her see what a mistake that would be,' said Percy earnestly. 'They are incompatible, but she cannot bring herself to break his heart. He is deeply in love with her, you know.'

A remark which should have given Louisa the greatest satisfaction, but didn't. She had wanted Helena to fall for Percy and free Thomas, but now, instead of freeing him from a girl she had decided wasn't the right wife for him, she was the means of hurting him. She said urgently, 'Then shouldn't you leave her alone to make sure that she's doing the right thing? You're taking advantage of him not being available to spend more time with her, aren't you?'

Percy gave her a searching look. 'I can't see that it's any business of yours.' He added pompously, 'I shall do as I think fit in the matter.'

She saw that she was going the wrong way about it.

'Are you going to Megan Woodley's wedding on Saturday? If you're not taking Helena, will you take me? I hate going by myself...'

Percy smiled. 'Well, well, so we're going to be friends again, are we, darling? As a matter of fact, Helena told me that she will be going with Gifford, so I'll escort you with pleasure. And if I slip away once in a while you will quite understand, won't you?'

Felicity had been listening idly, but now she asked, 'What shall you wear?'

'I haven't decided. I'll have to get a hat...'

There was no more talk of Helena; Felicity wanted to talk clothes, listening seriously to Percy's opinions. He fancied himself as an expert on women's fashions, and recommended that Louisa choose a subdued colour for her dress.

'You're a beautiful girl,' he told her in a patronising voice, 'but you must remember that you're what is vulgarly known as "well endowed".'

Louisa assured him that she would bear in mind his good advice, and later, back at her flat, combed through her wardrobe in search of something striking. She found what she wanted—a dress which she had bought last year and which, once she had got it home, she'd decided was a trifle too colourful. It was a black and white crêpe de Chine with a bold floral pattern and a pleated jabot falling from a low neckline. Not her at all; she wondered what on earth had possessed her to buy it.

But it would do nicely; Thomas wouldn't like it, and it would emphasise Helena's perfect taste. Percy wouldn't like it either, but that didn't matter in the least. She would get a large hat with an overpowering brim... The comparison would be very much in Helena's favour; Thomas would love her even more than he had done. 'And I,' said Louisa, talking to herself since there was no one else to talk to, 'will make sure that Percy doesn't get near Helena.'

The rest of the week was much as any other week; Louisa found time to buy a hat—an eye-catching black and white straw with a wide brim. She tried on the whole outfit and decided that Helena would be delighted when she saw it—and Percy had been right; the dress clung in all the wrong places.

Percy, very correctly dressed in his morning suit, arrived a little late on Saturday. The looks he cast her more than justified her expectations. He didn't say anything until they were arriving at the church, and then he said, 'Darling Louisa, you look gorgeous, but I must admit that the dress isn't quite you, and perhaps the hat could have been a shade smaller.' He smirked at her. 'Are you bidding for my attentions after all? I must tell you that, much as I love you, I have given my heart to Helena.'

'You sound like a Victorian melodrama,' said Louisa matter-of-factly. 'Let's go in before the bride arrives.'

It was a lovely church, the oldest in Salisbury, and it was almost full.

From her seat, Louisa looked carefully round her, peering with some difficulty from under the hat's brim, catching the eyes of friends and acquaintances, nodding and smiling until her eye lighted upon Thomas and Helena, sitting several pews ahead of her. But it wasn't until the congregation stood for the entry of the bride that she could get a good look at them.

Helena looked beautiful in an ice-blue outfit and a matching hat which framed her face to perfection. Thomas towered beside her, immaculate in a grey morning suit of impeccable cut. There was a rustle of silk and chiffon as the congregation seated itself again and the service began. Louisa didn't hear a word of it; she stood and sat and sang with everyone else and thought about Helena and Thomas getting married, aware that there was a stony sadness somewhere in her chest.

The bride and groom came down the aisle followed by the bridesmaids and the families and then more slowly the guests. It was inevitable that she and Percy should come face to face with Thomas and Helena and, in the dictates of politeness, exchange a few words.

Helena's words, uttered in a low, sweet voice, carried barbs.

'Louisa—such ages since we met. Did you have a good holiday? But I see that you did—so brown, and you've put on weight,' she trilled with gentle laughter. 'All that good Scottish porridge.'

Louisa smiled politely and watched Helena and Percy exchange glances, and then peeped at Thomas's face. He was watching them, too, but there was no expression on his face. He said all the right things in a placid manner and suggested that they should leave the church.

'We're bound to meet again at the reception,' he

observed pleasantly, and bore Helena off to the waiting car.

The reception was at the Woodleys' house, and since there were so many cars it took time to get there. Louisa kissed the bride, kissed the groom, too, since she had known him for years, and went to mingle with the guests, towing Percy with her. She hadn't seen Helena, but she didn't intend him to go looking for her.

For a time all went well. They drank champagne, ate morsels of this and that, talked to their many friends, and Percy made no move to go off on his own. The cake was cut, toasts made, and people began to stroll round the house and gardens while the bride and groom joined first one group and then another.

Louisa saw Helena and Thomas on the terrace, made sure that Percy was deep in conversation, and bent to admire the bride's ring. After a few leisurely moments she turned back to Percy. He wasn't there, nor was he to be seen. What was worse, Helena was no longer on the terrace, the doctor was walking towards her, and it was too late for flight.

He took her arm and walked her slowly away towards the rose garden at the further end of the lawn.

'I'm looking for Percy,' said Louisa, not at all her usual cool self. 'He can't be far away—he was here a minute ago...'

'I suspect that Witherspoon is quite capable of looking after himself.' He added calmly, 'He will be with Helena.' He glanced down at Louisa, unable to see her face because of the hat, but he was smiling.

'Well,' said Louisa, 'I must find him; I think it is time we left...'

'My dear Louisa, surely you know that no one goes

before the happy pair? Besides, you must allow
Helena and Percy a little time to themselves.'

She peered up at him from under the preposterous
brim. 'But they shouldn't—what I mean is, they don't
really—it's just that you are so often away and Helena
must get lonely. Besides, I think I may marry Percy
myself.'

The doctor suppressed a smile. 'You mustn't worry,
Louisa, I am quite capable of managing my own af-
fairs.'

She said snappily, 'I'm not worried. Why should I
worry? I hardly know you.' And then she added,
'Don't you mind?'

'No. Tell me, why are you dressed in that bunchy
frock and wearing that outsized hat? Almost as if you
wish to create the impression that you aren't in the
least attractive. Foolish Louisa, don't you know that
nothing you wear could dim your beauty? So why?'

'Helena is so beautiful; I wanted her to look love-
lier than anyone else here.' Louisa was aware that she
hadn't explained very clearly, but the doctor seemed
to understand.

'Ah, yes, of course. She does look particularly
lovely today, doesn't she?'

Louisa said 'Yes,' in small voice, then added, 'We
should go back to the house...'

And then, because she couldn't help herself, she
asked, 'When are you getting married?'

He was strolling along beside her, very much at
ease.

'That is for the bride to decide.'

'I suppose so.' They walked on slowly and she tried
to think of something to say, but all she was thinking
of were the days they had spent together at Shieldaig,
and on no account must they be mentioned.

As they neared the house she could see Helena talking with several people, but there was no sign of Percy.

'There's Helena,' said Louisa unnecessarily. 'I expect she's been looking for you. I'll find Percy.'

She had a sudden wish to tell him that she wasn't going to marry Percy—not even if he was the last man on earth. Instead she said soberly, 'Goodbye, Thomas,' and walked away very fast.

Percy was unusually quiet as they drove back to Salisbury. Beyond remarking that it had been a charming wedding and what a pity that Louisa had chosen to wear that particular outfit, he had little to say. At her flat she asked him if he wanted a cup of coffee, only to be told that he had too much on his mind to be sociable.

'Probably too much in your stomach as well,' said Louisa. 'Thanks for taking me to the wedding. I should have an early night if I were you.'

'Sleep is out of the question,' said Percy pompously. 'You are a very unsympathetic girl, Louisa. I am only just beginning to realise that.'

He drove away before she could think of an answer.

The flat was warm and stuffy, so she opened all the windows, changed into a cotton dress, made a pot of tea and then gave the whole place a good clean because the idea of sitting down to read or watch television was suddenly unattractive. Tomorrow, she decided, she would get up early and drive to Stalbridge and spend the day with Aunt Martha. She was sure of a welcome, and the old lady would relish a good gossip about the wedding.

It was a dull morning, but still very warm. Louisa, driving down to Stalbridge with almost no traffic on the roads at such an early hour, allowed her thoughts to wander to the wedding. It seemed to her that she had failed to interest Percy in herself, but that didn't seem to matter, for the doctor didn't appear to be at all alarmed at the deepening friendship between Helena and Percy.

'So I need not do anything more about it,' said Louisa, talking to herself as usual. 'I expect he'll whisk her away and marry her out of hand when he's good and ready.' The thought brought her no satisfaction; Helena would make him unhappy. She swallowed the sad little lump in her throat and thought about something else, only not very successfully.

Aunt Martha was, as usual, pleased to see her.

'My dear, this is nice. I've just this minute made coffee and put a nice little piece of lamb in the oven. We'll sit down and you shall tell me about the wedding. The Woodleys are such nice people; one would wish them every happiness.'

The sun was still behind thin clouds, and they sat in the small sitting room, the coffee tray between them, and presently Aunt Martha asked, 'You had a good holiday with Bob and Kitty? Thank you for your card, dear; it reminded me of the visits I paid there years ago. And what did you do with yourself all day?'

She looked at Louisa with her mild brown eyes, the picture of casual interest, while Kitty's letter—page after page of information about Thomas—sat snugly in her handbag. Kitty had suggested that the doctor's interest in Louisa was rather more than casual, but that Louisa showed no signs of being in love. So now Aunt Martha began asking questions, carefully wrapped up in such a way that Louisa took them to be idle curiosity.

'He sounds rather a nice man,' said Aunt Martha mildly.

'Well, yes, he is, most of the time. We don't always see eye to eye.'

'Life would be very dull if we agreed with each other all the time,' pronounced her aunt. 'Fetch the sherry and the glasses, child; we will have a drink before lunch.'

Driving back to Salisbury that evening, Louisa planned the week ahead. She would go and see Felicity, of course, and if she could get some extra time at lunch one day she would do some shopping. She needed a dress, something pretty, just one, in case Percy—or any of the men of her acquaintance— should ask her out. And she had promised to drive down to Southampton one evening to see an old school friend, not long married and with a first baby. There was plenty to fill her leisure, she decided.

Monday was busy at the consulting rooms and Sir James was rather crusty. There was no sign of Thomas, although she really hadn't expected him. All the same, she was conscious of disappointment, although she didn't know why she should feel it; she certainly didn't have the time to think about it.

Sir James was still at his desk when she and Mrs Grant and Jilly prepared to leave, and he called her back at the last minute to rearrange some of his appointments so that the other two had already gone. In a hurry to get away before Sir James could find something else for her to do, she nipped across the waiting room and opened the door, to run full tilt into Thomas's waistcoat. It was like hitting a tree trunk, and she almost tumbled over.

'My goodness,' said Louisa. 'Are you made of solid rock?'

He had set her tidily back on her feet, but he still had a hand on her arm.

He said quietly, 'No, Louisa, I am just as any other man—flesh and blood and human feelings.' He took his hand away and went unhurriedly to the consulting room, and she stood, feeling bewildered, watching his broad back disappear through the door. The bewilderment gave place to something else, though. A great surge of feeling which took her breath.

'How silly,' whispered Louisa, 'to fall in love with a man when he's walked away without even looking back.'

She went slowly out into the street and started to walk to the flat. Of course, now she came to think about it, she had loved him for a long time, only she hadn't allowed herself to own up to it. Not that it would have made any difference.

The doctor, standing at the window, watched her go. Only when she was out of sight did he turn round.

'I'm sorry, I missed that—you were saying…?'

Sir James looked at him over his glasses. 'Of course, it's none of my business, Thomas, but you should get married, you know.'

Thomas said, unsmiling, 'Yes, I have come to that conclusion, too.' He added, 'But the waiting has been to some purpose…'

Sir James, not quite sure what he meant, and being a wise man, changed the subject.

Sir James had no patients on the following morning and saw no reason why Louisa shouldn't have an extra hour at lunchtime. He would be at the hospital until the early afternoon, and since the last patient that day had an appointment for five o'clock Louisa guessed that she would have to stay later than usual. Not that it mattered; the busier she was, the better, because then there wasn't time to think about Thomas. She gobbled her sandwiches, drank a too hot cup of tea and went off to the shops she had decided to visit. A dress she could wear at any time, anywhere, and perhaps some new sandals—the useless kind with high heels and complicated straps.

She found two dresses which were exactly what she wanted so she bought them both. One was straw-coloured washed silk, elegantly cut and expensive, and the other a cotton dress, very pale blue, with a vague pattern of tiny flowers. Satisfied with her purchases, she went to the shoe shop at the corner of the arcade and found just what she wanted there—straw-coloured sandals in soft leather, high-heeled and strappy. Resisting the temptation to buy a handbag which took her fancy, she left the shop and found Helena waiting for her.

'Louisa, I saw you as I was passing, and it's so long since we had a chat.' She glanced at the plastic bags Louisa was carrying. 'Shopping? Something nice? You looked very striking at the wedding—not at all your usual style, but eye-catching. Were you trying to get Percy back?'

Louisa said coolly, 'What makes you think that he ever went? But, no, I don't want him.' She smiled widely. 'You can have him, Helena.'

Helena went red. 'What a ridiculous thing to say. You forget, I'm engaged to marry Thomas Gifford. And you have no right to talk like that about Percy; he is a most sensitive man. We have a great deal in common, he is an ideal companion, and we agree about so much…'

'Now it is you who is forgetting Thomas.'

Helena narrowed her eyes. 'I intend to marry Thomas. I shall make him a good wife, help him in his career, and run his home. I shall make the best of the frequent absences he makes. He's been away recently on some consultation or other. If it hadn't been for Percy's kindness, I should have been lonely.'

'What twaddle you do talk,' said Louisa briskly. 'Thomas already has a career—he certainly doesn't need any help from you—and Rosie runs his home to perfection. And, now, I really must go. I said I'd be back by one-thirty.'

Helena laid a hand on her arm. 'Just a minute— you seem to know an awful lot about Thomas.'

Louisa smiled into the beautiful, cross face. 'You forget, he's by way of being a partner to Sir James. I work for Sir James…'

She glanced again at her watch. 'I really must fly.' She flung a goodbye over her shoulder as she went, wondering what Helena would say if she knew Thomas had been at Shieldaig. She had been tempted to tell her, but if Thomas hadn't told her himself it was hardly for her to do so. Besides, she wanted to keep those few days by the loch a secret. She had been happy then, although she hadn't known why, and they were all she had to remember Thomas by.

She saw him again the next day and, beyond a brief greeting and an equally brief report on Lucky, he had nothing to say to her. In any case the front she presented as Miss Howarth, efficient and reserved receptionist, precluded any gesture of friendliness. Sir James called her in with some patients' notes he wished to discuss with Thomas, and she took care not to look at him when she laid them on Sir James's desk. But she hadn't needed to take precautions against meeting him for he took no notice of her then, and, when he went away presently, he looked at her as though she was someone he had met and instantly forgotten.

She went to see Felicity that evening and found her alone.

'Darling, how nice. I'm so bored all by myself. Almost everyone I know is away on holiday and those who aren't only want to play bridge, and one can get tired of bridge. Pour me a drink and tell me all the gossip.'

Which really meant that Felicity did the gossiping, tearing her dear friends to shreds, recounting titbits of news, and then reporting with a wealth of detail a visit she had made to the dentist.

Louisa listened and smiled and murmured because she knew that Felicity really was lonely, and presently she asked, 'Is Percy away, too?'

'He might just as well be. I hardly see him these days, and when he is here he does nothing but eulogise about Helena Thornfold. I think I might go away myself.'

'Why not? I'll keep an eye on this place, and Biddy can have her holiday at the same time.'

'What a good idea, then I shan't be inconvenienced at all. I'll think where I want to go and let you know.'

Louisa got up to go. 'I'll go and see Biddy on my way out. Tell me when you've arranged something.'

In the kitchen Biddy plied her with strong tea and a slice of the cake she had just taken from the oven. Her sharp eyes peered into Louisa's face.

'Still looking peaky. You don't get enough fun. You ought to be out every night with some young man, miss. That Mr Witherspoon who was so keen on you—we don't see 'im no more, or 'ardly ever.' She refilled Louisa's cup. 'And I'll tell you something, but not a word to anyone—promise?'

'I promise. Has someone at the pub been misbehaving themselves?'

Biddy shook her head. 'This is serious, Miss Louisa, so you listen careful. This Miss Thornfold your Mr Witherspoon's so crazy about—well, 'im and 'er are going to marry.'

'Biddy, what nonsense! She's engaged to Dr Gifford; I saw her only yesterday.'

'That's as may be. This is gospel truth. Mrs Watts' sister works for the Thornfolds, and she 'appened ter 'ear Miss Thornfold and Mr Witherspoon talking. Well, she was actually by the door and they'd left it open. Ever so dramatic they were, she said, talking about duty and the call of love and I don't know what else. Anyway, they're going off—secret, like—on Saturday afternoon, pretending they're going off ter 'ave lunch with friends, but they've got a special licence and are going ter some church—funny name it was, too—Ebbes-something.'

'Ebbesborne Wake,' said Louise. 'Biddy, do you suppose Mrs Watts has imagined all this?'

'Lor' bless you, no, miss. Why, she goes to chapel each Sunday. She told me because we're friends and I'm telling you because you've always been good ter me and you ought to know about that Mr Witherspoon.'

'Do you think anyone else knows, Biddy?'

'Not a whisper. Miss, do you suppose it'll turn out OK?'

'I don't know, Biddy.' Louisa smiled at her companion. 'But things often come right, don't they? I must go; it's quite late and we've a busy morning tomorrow.'

She kissed the little woman, let herself out of the kitchen door and walked home. Once there she made yet another pot of tea and sat down to think. Something must be done before Thomas had his heart broken...

CHAPTER NINE

LOUISA sat for a long time, a mug of cooling tea in her hand, wondering what was best to be done. She was aware that she intended to interfere again, but this time it was for the best of reasons. That Thomas was making the mistake of his life in marrying Helena she was quite sure, but if he loved her that surely was more important than anything else. The thing was to prevent Percy and Helena getting married on Saturday. Even if it meant only a delay, it would give Thomas time to talk to Helena. It was a pity Biddy didn't know the time of the ceremony; a calculated guess would have to do. They intended to tell everyone that they were lunching with friends—that meant any time between twelve o'clock and two o'clock.

'If I get to the church by midday…' mused Louisa. She had no idea what she would say or do after that, but that wasn't important. A pity that Thomas couldn't be warned—it would be the sensible thing to do—but Biddy had made her promise not to tell anyone. There was the chance, thought Louisa hopefully, that he might get to hear of it. There were two days yet before Saturday; anything could happen.

But nothing did. He came to the consulting rooms on the following afternoon, politely remote, looking unworried, went to the hospital with Sir James, came back and was closeted with him for the rest of the afternoon. And Louisa, taking letters in to be signed, heard him telling Sir James that he was taking Helena to the theatre at Chichester that evening.

So he could have no inkling of Helena and Percy's plans. Perhaps Helena would tell him that she was going to marry Percy; it seemed the sensible thing to do. Louisa couldn't see the point of all the secrecy. Surely Helena wasn't being deliberately unkind? Thinking about it, she decided that that was quite likely. But why? To pay him back for all the times he had been unable to take her out, all the times he had had to leave her at a party, or phone at the last minute to say that he had an urgent call?

More than likely, decided Louisa, going home to cook her supper.

There was a pile of ironing waiting to be done; she tidied away her meal, got out the ironing board and began on the basketful of washing. She was halfway through it, listening anxiously to the distant rumble of thunder, when the doorbell was rung. It was probably Mrs Watts wanting to borrow milk or tea or sugar—frequently the case—but whether it was loneliness or erratic housekeeping, Louisa had been unable to discover. She switched off the iron and went to open the door.

The doctor stood outside, leaning against the wall.

'I make a habit of this, don't I?' he wanted to know cheerfully.

'You should be at Chichester,' said Louisa. She spoke severely, but her heart raced with delight. 'Why aren't you?'

And, since she couldn't leave him outside, she added, 'Come in, do.'

'I'm always so sure of a welcome,' murmured Thomas, and went past her into the sitting room. 'I got called away shortly before we were leaving. Luckily Helena phoned Witherspoon, who most obligingly took my place.'

Louisa opened her mouth to say something, thought better of it, and shut it again.

'I wondered if we might go somewhere and have a meal or a drink?' He had gone to the window to look at the darkening sky.

'I've had my supper,' said Louisa sedately. 'Thank you all the same.'

'Then a drink?' He sounded friendly but hardly eager.

'Well, no, thank you. There's going to be a storm, and I'd rather be here...'

'Frightened?' There was no mockery in his voice.

'Yes. I can sit here and look at the wall and be as cowardly as I like.'

'Well, you can sit here and look at me instead, or keep your eyes shut and your hands over your ears if you wish; I shan't mind. Why not finish the ironing while I make coffee?'

So she switched on the iron again, since he obviously intended to stay for a while, and if she had something to do it would be easier...

He talked to her while he was in the kitchen, a gentle medley of the day's happenings; Bellow, Lucky, Rosie cutting her finger on the bread knife...commonplace chat which was soothing and which made no mention of Helena.

And don't let him start on her, prayed Louisa silently, because I might let something slip. She still had no idea how things would turn out; she might be successful in stopping the marriage, but that was only the beginning. Hopefully, Helena might come to her senses—after all, she would be giving up a lot if she married Percy...

'Why do you frown so fiercely at the ironing board?' asked Thomas, coming in with the tray.

She was saved from answering by a flash of lightning and a peal of thunder much too close for her peace of mind. She squeaked 'Oh,' and switched off the iron with a hand which shook a little. 'Sorry, I told you I was a coward.'

He said quietly, 'Come and sit here, away from the window; the storm's going over quite rapidly.' He poured the coffee and handed her a cup. 'I found the biscuit tin!'

Another flash filled the room with vivid blue light. 'Oh,' said Louisa again, sitting rigid while the thunder banged and crashed overhead. 'What a good thing you came here instead of driving straight back.'

Of course, that was why he had come, knowing that there was a bad storm brewing and prudently taking shelter.

Thomas, watching her tell-tale expression, smiled to himself.

The storm stayed overhead for some time, fading away and then returning with renewed vigour. The doctor made a second pot of coffee and, without being asked, a plate of buttered toast spread with Marmite, aware that doing something normal like eating and drinking was soothing to the nerves. Of course, he would have preferred to gather Louisa into his arms— an agreeable alternative which required all his self-control to deny. He had the patience to wait.

The storm rolled away at last, muttering in the distance, taking the lightning with it.

'Time I went,' said Thomas, gathering up the cups and plates. 'Finish that bit of ironing while I tidy up.'

He went to the window. 'The moon's coming up and the stars are out; it will be a quiet night.'

He wandered off into the kitchen and she listened to him whistling as he washed up. It all seems so right, she reflected unhappily, us like this—comfortable with each other. And to think that I didn't like him much.

She was folding the last handkerchief when he came back into the room.

'Thanks for the coffee,' he said. 'I'm going to Winchester tomorrow so I won't see you until next week. I'll be in on Tuesday morning.'

'Will you be staying at Winchester?' Supposing he didn't come back to Salisbury until Tuesday? He wouldn't know about Helena and Percy.

'I wouldn't imagine so.' She could hear that he wasn't going to say more than that and she had no chance to say more, even if she could have thought of something to say, for he wished her goodnight and went away.

Louisa stared at the door for quite some time before it struck her that she was wasting time thinking about Thomas when she should be planning what she would do on Saturday.

She and Mrs Grant and Jilly took it in turns to go to the consulting rooms each Saturday morning, just to make sure that everything had been locked up and shut off until Monday. It didn't take long; the answering machine to check, the post to take in, make sure that the gas had been turned off—a routine which was largely unnecessary, but to which they faithfully adhered.

It was her turn to go in this Saturday. That didn't matter as long as she got away in time to arrive at Ebbesborne Wake by about half past twelve. Percy and Helena weren't likely to be there much before one o'clock, the normal lunch hour. Unless, of course, they had said that they were lunching with friends some way away. It was a risk she would have to take. Better be on the safe side and get there by noon....

Friday seemed to go on for ever. She exchanged hopes for a pleasant weekend with her colleagues and hurried home. There would be no time to do the usual weekend shopping in the morning; she hurried to a grocery store, stocked up rapidly and went back to lay out everything she would need in the morning. And when she had done that she sat down and wondered if she was doing the right thing. But there was nothing else to do. Thomas wasn't there even if she broke her word to Biddy; he must at least have the chance to try and win Helena back. Louisa, feeling as if she were entangled in a Gothic novel, went to bed.

It was raining in the morning. Louisa ate a hurried breakfast and went along to the consulting rooms where she did the small chores expected of her. It was still only mid-morning when she was ready to leave, and she was getting into her mac when the door opened and Sir James came in.

He looked pleased to see her. 'Splendid, just the person I wanted to see. There are a couple of letters to send to Professor Lutvik. I'll dictate them at once and you can type them and get them off.'

Louisa, half in and half out of her mac, said urgently, 'Sir, I've an appointment for twelve o'clock which I must keep...'

'You'll be done long before then, Miss Howarth. The letters are brief—ten minutes or so should be enough.'

It was half an hour, because Sir James changed his mind when he had dictated the first letter and she had to start all over again. And the second one wasn't short at all, and full of long words. When at length they were done, signed and stamped, she saw with horror that it was already half past eleven.

'Pop them in the post,' said Sir James genially. 'You'll catch the midday posting time if you hurry. Run along, now, you don't need to dawdle around any longer.'

Louisa, speechless, could only mutter goodbye. She would have to go to the post office if she was to catch the noon posting. She almost ran there, and then hurried back to get her car from the garage at her stepmother's house. And all the time the minutes ticked away.

Ebbesborne Wake wasn't far away from Salisbury as the crow flew, but she wasn't a crow and the roads were narrow. For a fuming ten minutes she was forced to creep along behind a load of hay until at last she was able to turn into another narrow lane leading to the village and the church. It was half past twelve by now, and still raining steadily. She drove past the pub and parked the car outside the church. There was no car there and her heart sank until she remembered that they had probably not arrived yet.

The church was small, very old and smelled of generations of damp and chill, but it was beautiful and peaceful. There was no one there. She walked down its aisle and peeped into the vestry, which was empty, and then, undecided as to what to do next, hesitated by the front pew.

'Don't let me be too late!' said Louisa, who had an old-fashioned belief in prayers being answered. And hers was. The church door creaked open and an elderly parson came in. He saw her at once and came down the aisle.

'I'm afraid you are too late if you have come for the wedding. Were you not told that they had changed

the time from one o'clock to half past ten? Something
to do with catching their plane. They explained that
was why there were no guests. There was no time to
warn them. Really, one is at the mercy of public ser-
vices these days. Is that your car outside? I hope you
haven't come too far?'

'No,' said Louisa. 'Only from Salisbury. I hoped
I'd be in time.'

'So tiresome, and such bad weather.' He hesitated.
'I have come to close the church...'

'Of course. I'll go.' Louisa summoned a smile, although she wanted to weep.

She went out of the church, got into her car and
followed the lane round the hill until it joined the road
again. She was almost there when the Bentley passed
her. The lane was narrow; she had ample time to see
Thomas at the wheel. She didn't stop to wonder why
he was there but joined the road, turned back into the
lane again and stopped once more outside the church.
The Bentley was, she saw, already there.

'Over here, Louisa,' said Thomas, leaning back
against an ancient tombstone.

Words came tumbling out before she reached him.

'Thomas, oh, Thomas, I'm sorry. They're married
already. I was going to get here first... Sir James kept
me... I never meant, at least, I didn't think...'

These fragments of information appeared to leave
the doctor unmoved. He said placidly, 'Come here,
Louisa, and sit down.' He patted the ancient flat tombstone beside him. 'Get your breath and tell me at your
leisure why you are so bothered.'

'Of course I'm bothered.' She huddled onto the
tombstone. 'There's no time to explain; perhaps you
could go after them.'

'And if by any chance I should find them, what do you suppose I should do?'

'How should I know?' She was almost in tears.

'In that case, let us sit here peacefully while you explain.'

'You will be very angry.'

'Let us not make any futile conjectures about my state of mind until I am in possession of the facts.' He joined her on the tombstone. 'Now, supposing you begin at the beginning? Keeping, if possible, to the facts.'

'But aren't you going after them? To get an explanation?' Louisa stopped herself just in time from wringing her hands. 'I expect you're in a state of shock...'

The doctor somehow or other managed not to smile. 'All the more reason to be put in possession of the truth. You implied that this marriage is your fault.'

'Well, it is.' Louisa blew her nose—an alternative to bursting into tears. 'You won't interrupt, will you?'

'No, no.'

'Well,' began Louisa, and then stopped. 'How did you know? It was a secret.'

'These things get around,' he said casually, and then added, 'I'm waiting.'

'It's all my fault,' said Louisa in a sudden rush of words. 'You see, I thought that Helena and Percy were so suited to each other.' She gulped. 'And I didn't think she was the right wife for you, so I thought that if they met and liked each other...' Once she started she didn't stop; it all came pouring out, sometimes muddled, but she didn't leave anything out.

'And then I was told that they were going to get married, and I had to do something about it, but I didn't know what. You see, I had to stop them if I could. I didn't know that you loved Helena, you see. At least, I thought you loved her a bit, otherwise you wouldn't have asked her to marry you, but I didn't know that you were deeply in love with her.'

She gave a sudden gulp. 'I've ruined your love life and I don't know what to do about it.'

She blew her nose again, and didn't see Thomas's delighted grin. He was enjoying himself hugely, and once Louisa had talked herself out he would enjoy himself even more...

His phone rang and he took it from his pocket. He listened for a moment, and then said, 'I'm on my way—twenty minutes or so.'

He put the phone back in his pocket. He wasn't a man who swore habitually but now he did, in a harsh voice which caused Louisa to look at him in surprise.

'I must go at once. Get in the car and come with me, Louisa.'

She shook her head. 'No, I'd rather not. I don't think I want to see you again, and I'm sure you feel the same.

He didn't answer, and she watched him drive away seconds later.

She stayed sitting on the tombstone for a long time. It had been a relief to tell him everything but it hadn't helped in any way. Helena and Percy were married, and even if Helena changed her mind—and divorce was easy—it would take some time to sort things out. Louisa would have to go away, of course, at least leave her job. Thomas wouldn't be able to bear the sight of her.

Louisa, who hadn't cried, burst into tears and sat snivelling and sniffing, and the rain which had held off for a while started a steady drizzle. She didn't notice, nor did she care.

It was very quiet. The church stood a little apart from the village and the pub had its doors closed. Saturday afternoon and everyone was indoors watching sport on the television. Louisa leaned her head against a moss-covered headstone hanging over the tomb and closed her eyes. She was unhappy—she had never been so unhappy in her life before—and her head ached and she was tired. She closed her eyes and, heedless of the rain and the hardness of her resting place, went to sleep.

She woke hours later, to find the doctor in a white-hot rage standing over her. 'Good God, girl, are you mad?' he wanted to know.

He had spent hours at the hospital, carefully piecing together the fragments of a small girl's broken leg as only he could do it, but, that done to his satisfaction, he had driven round to Louisa's flat and found no one there. He had tried her stepmother's house, too, and Felicity, on her way to early-evening drinks, had told him airily that she hadn't any idea where Louisa was. Nor had Biddy been able to help. He didn't know what had decided him to drive to Ebbesborne Wake, and now finding her there, sitting where he had left her, left him shaking with anger.

The anger went as swiftly as it had come. He said gently, 'Did you go to sleep? You're very wet. Come along; I'll take you home.'

Louisa sat up. 'I can't, I've got pins and needles.' Then she said, 'I can manage; my car's in the lane. I'll go home now.'

He scooped her off the tombstone and carried her to his car.

'I'm too heavy,' said Louisa. He didn't bother to

answer but shovelled her into the front seat, got in beside her and drove off.

'My car?' said Louisa. The sleep had refreshed her and her spirits had lifted.

'Someone can fetch it.'

Presently she said, 'We're going the wrong way.'

'Allow me to know my own way home.' He didn't sound angry any more.

'Not to your house?' said Louisa urgently.

'You need to wash your face and get those wet things off, and we both need a meal.'

'I can do that at home.'

He didn't answer and she sat silently, wishing that she wasn't there beside him, and at the same time happy to be with him, even if he was in a towering rage.

There was no sign of ill humour as he stopped before his front door. He bustled her inside, and Rosie came to meet them in the hall. She showed no surprise at the sight of Louisa, merely tut-tutted in a soothing way, remarking on the nasty rain, and took the mac the doctor had peeled off Louisa.

'And those shoes, miss. They've had a proper soaking—wet feet and all. You just come along to the cloakroom and I'll have those stockings off you.'

She bore Louisa away, saying over her shoulder, 'I'll have a pot of tea for you in ten minutes, sir.'

The doctor took his bag to his study and went to the drawing room to be greeted by Bellow and Lucky. He sat down in his chair; his work had taught him patience, and he was content to wait.

Louisa came presently, her face pale with fright, her damp hair tied back with a piece of string from her pocket. She was a practical girl, and one never knew when a piece of string would come in handy.

Her beautiful nose was pink-tipped and her eyes were puffy and shadowed. Her dress, crumpled and stained from the ancient stone upon which she had sat, did nothing for her appearance.

The doctor set the kitten gently upon the carpet and got to his feet.

'Come and sit down,' he invited, his voice friendly and casual. 'Rosie is bringing tea, and presently we'll have a meal.'

'No,' said Louisa. 'That is, no, thank you. I'd like to go home as soon as it's convenient. I've been more than enough trouble.' She sniffed, and he got up again and offered her a perfectly laundered handkerchief.

'It's not convenient,' he told her placidly. 'Certainly you have been a trouble, but that I can overlook for I'm sure your intentions were well-meant.'

'They were, only they went wrong.' She didn't look at him; the kitten had climbed onto her lap and she was stroking it. 'What will you do? Is there anything I can do to put it right?'

'I don't intend to do anything. It is only fair to let you know that I am delighted that Helena and Witherspoon are married. I was a little worried that something might occur to prevent that.'

She did look at him then. 'But that's not... You can't mean...?'

Rosie coming in with the tea tray prevented her from saying more, which was just as well, since she had been saying nothing to the point.

She poured the tea and, since she was very hungry even if her heart was breaking, she ate the sandwiches and cake which Rosie had thoughtfully provided. She wiped the last crumb from her mouth and got to her feet.

'Thank you for my tea; you have been very kind. Do you suppose...?'

'I suppose nothing, Louisa. Sit down and listen to me. Do you imagine that you were the only one to realise how suitable Helena and Witherspoon were together? All they needed was a little encouragement and a chance to see as much of each other as possible. It was inevitable, even without your well-meant schemes.'

'But she told Percy that she couldn't marry him because you loved her so much and it would break your heart.'

'My dear girl, what woman, given the chance, isn't going to make the most of such a situation? Percy had not the least idea of what my feelings might have been, but such a remark would only have served to clinch the matter between them. I rather think that they will be happy together, just as we shall be happy...'

Louisa looked at him, sitting in his chair so calmly, saying things like that as though he was discussing the weather. She said uncertainly, 'I don't quite understand.'

'I fell in love with you when we met. I knew what I wanted—I wanted you for my wife—but, of course, that had to wait while the situation was sorted out. I saw the solution when I saw Helena and Witherspoon together, and after that it was merely a question of time.'

He got out of his chair, pulled her to her feet and held her close. 'So you see, my darling, this was destined to happen even without your efforts. If I had known that you were going to race off to Ebbesborne Wake in that impetuous fashion, I would have stopped you.'

'But you didn't know.'

'Oh, but I did. Biddy wrote me a letter.'

Louisa stared up at him. 'She did? But it was a secret…'

'She thought that I should know. You see, she was so certain that you loved me.'

Louisa, an honest girl, said, 'Yes, I do. That's why I wanted Helena and Percy to meet, but I didn't know then, if you see what I mean. I wasn't sure if I liked you, only I knew that she was all wrong for you.'

An observation which afforded the doctor a good deal of satisfaction.

'Say that again.'

'That's why I wanted…'

'No, no. The first bit.'

She felt his arms tighten around her. It was a delightful sensation.

'Oh, you mean when I said "Yes, I do".' She added, 'I do love you, Thomas.'

He kissed her then, very gently, and then with a most satisfying ruthlessness.

Louisa sighed in his arms. 'Do you suppose that Helena and Percy will be happy?'

'I see no reason why they shouldn't be.' He kissed the top of her untidy head. 'Not, of course, as happy as we shall be.'

He smiled at her with such tenderness that for a moment she thought that she might cry with happiness. 'We shall have an ideal marriage,' said Thomas. 'We shall love each other and argue and quarrel and make it up again and delight in each other's company. And the children, of course.'

'Little boys,' said Louisa dreamily.

'Little girls, too.'

'If you say so, dear Thomas,' said Louisa. She smiled at him so sweetly that he kissed her again.

If you enjoyed what you just read,
then we've got an offer you can't resist!

Take 2 bestselling
love stories FREE!
Plus get a FREE surprise gift!

Finding Home

New York Times bestselling authors

Linda Howard
Elizabeth Lowell
Kasey Michaels

invite you on
the journey of a lifetime.

Three women are searching—
each wants a place to belong,
a man to care for her,
a child to love.

Will her wishes be fulfilled?

*Coming in April 2001
only from Silhouette Books!*

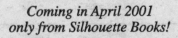

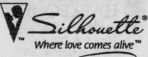